It had taken Adam long enough to find where he belonged....

No one—especially not a woman with no ties to family or land—would come between him and the dreams God had called him home to.

Adam didn't need or want his life turned inside out by a stubborn woman who didn't believe in promises, or God, or slowing down long enough to see exactly what she was missing. A loner like himself had no business tying anyone else down to his obligations.

Keeping Lisa around in the confines of his lodge was definitely asking for trouble. Regardless of her familial connections or her charming personality, the beautiful drifter couldn't stay. Wouldn't, even if he'd be foolish enough to ask her to...

Books by Carol Steward

Love Inspired

There Comes a Season #27
Her Kind of Hero #56
Courting Katarina #134
This Time Forever #165

CAROL STEWARD

wrote daily to a pen pal for ten years, yet writing as a career didn't occur to her for another two decades. "My first key chain said, 'Bloom where you're planted.' I've tried to follow that advice ever since."

Carol, her husband and their three children have planted their roots in Greeley. Together, their family enjoys sports, camping and discovering Colorado's beauty. Carol has operated her own cake-decorating business and spent fifteen years providing full-time child care to more than one hundred children before moving on to the other end of the education field. She is now an admissions adviser at a state university.

As always, Carol loves to hear from her readers. You can contact her at P.O. Box 5021, Greeley, CO 80632. She would also love for you to visit her Web page at http://members.aol.com/csteward37.

This Time Forever

Carol Steward

Love Inspired®

Published by Steeple Hill Books™

STEEPLE HILL BOOKS

Steeple
Hill™

ISBN 0-373-87172-4

THIS TIME FOREVER

Copyright © 2002 by Carol Steward

Visit us at www.steeplehill.com

Printed in U.S.A.

And He said to them, "Come away by yourselves
to a lonely place, and rest a while."
—*Mark* 6:31

Acknowledgments

I'd like to acknowledge my husband, Dave,
and my three kids, Sarah, Matthew and Scott.
It's not always easy having a writer for a wife
and mother, yet they keep encouraging me,
even when the going gets tough. Thanks.

And a special thank-you
to my editor, Melissa Endlich,
for her patience and understanding,
and the faith that I would finish this book.

Dedication

To my two Dads: Tom Bohannon and Jack Steward.
Wow, we really miss you!

Prologue

Lisa Berthoff watched the quarter-size flakes of snow swirl in the darkness as her sister and brother-in-law drove away for their honeymoon. Guests left and family hurried around, cleaning up after the wedding and reception. No one wanted to be stranded at the church. The blizzard had dumped twelve inches in the three hours since they had arrived.

On her way up the stairs to the bridal suite, she glanced at the bride's bouquet, caught in the crystal chandelier. "That could only have happened to Katarina," she said with a chuckle.

Adam MacIntyre, the groom's youngest brother added, "It's becoming a family trait, getting the bouquet caught on something."

Lisa smiled. "Oh, yeah. Emily's caught in the tree—I forgot about that. Guess I was only concerned with how to avoid catching it." Lisa had been expecting Katarina to throw the bouquet to her or Adam since they were the only unmarried siblings left.

"You're not superstitious, are you? That was only a coincidence."

"Superstitious? Not me, but I saw you hiding across the room." Lisa laughed. "Don't tell me you weren't half expecting our families to set us up. First Emily and Kevin caught a bouquet, and six months later they're married. Five months later Alex and Katarina catch Emily's bouquet, and eight months later—"

"Doesn't matter now, does it?" He motioned toward the chandelier. "We're free from the wedding curse. What do we need to finish up here? Since Kevin had a car full of people, and the rest of the family went to their hotels, I agreed to make sure you get home okay before I leave."

Lisa had convinced her mother and eldest sister, Emily, that she could make it to Katarina's house without a problem. Leave it to them to arrange for an escort. "I just need to load the cake into Katarina's van and get my things from upstairs. I won't be long. You can go on home."

"Katarina and Alex's house is on my way out of town. Besides, I don't think Kat's van is going anywhere on these roads. I'll take care of the cake."

Lisa ran upstairs, gathered her things and put them into her bag. She caught a glimpse of herself in the mirror, and paused. She swayed back and forth, watching the fabric move in fluid motion, then spun on one foot and watched the dress fan out and swirl around her legs.

"Katarina's quite a seamstress. All three of you looked beautiful in your dresses."

Lisa turned. She swallowed a lump of embarrassment at being caught doing something so childish. Adam was leaning against the door frame with his arms crossing his chest. The MacIntyre men looked handsome as ever in their tuxes. Adam was no exception. "Thank you. You and your brothers clean up pretty nicely yourselves." She turned to find her purse. "I thought you were taking the cake to the van."

"Pastor Mike had already taken care of it. I thought I'd better see if you had anything else to carry down. Mike doesn't think his car will make it, so I offered to give him a ride home, too."

After a quick glance to make sure she had everything, Lisa slipped into the leather coat Katarina had loaned her. "Sorry for the delay." She felt her cheeks heat up again and grabbed her purse.

"Not a problem. I rather enjoyed watching your little dance."

She faced Adam, waiting for him to move out of the way. "It was terribly rude of you not to let me know you were there."

"Did you expect me to join you?"

She tried to take her eyes off his dark brown gaze and his wide smile. "Dream on. My boyfriend would not appreciate me dancing with someone else, even if you and I are practically related.''

"Then again, he's not here, is he?"

Lisa tried to get past Adam. "We're keeping the pastor waiting."

Adam chuckled. "Pastor's going to have a long wait if he's waiting on me. I dodged that bouquet."

"You are a true cad," she said, pushing her way past him. "If you think I was implying…" She stopped and spun around to face him again. "I didn't…" Lisa lifted her finger to lecture him, then decided it wasn't worth the effort and continued down the stairs.

Adam followed. "Everyone knows this MacIntyre will avoid the altar at all costs."

"Doesn't appear to be an immediate problem, does it?" Lisa snapped, picking up her pace.

"You ought to talk." Adam smiled.

Lisa ignored his remark.

Pastor Mike looked up as Lisa and Adam made their way down the stairs. "I need to go get my briefcase from my car. I'll meet you at your truck." Mike opened the door and stepped outside. A strong gust of wind blew past them, rattling the chandelier.

Lisa sucked in a breath of icy air and closed her eyes. When she opened them, she saw the bridal bouquet blow loose, right into her hands.

Lisa ducked as another piece flew past her and hit Adam in the chest.

Lisa stared at the bouquet in horror.

"Not superstitious, huh? Tell you what," Adam suggested. "Let's keep this *our* little secret."

"Keep what a secret?" Lisa countered. She tossed the bouquet on the stairs. "I didn't see a thing."

Chapter One

One Year Later

Lisa Berthoff switched the cellular phone to her other ear and eased the sporty rental car to the shoulder of Highway 1.

"Lisa, Francie here. I need you in Colorado to do the story on a bed-and-breakfast. We're backlogged for weeks. Your ticket's waiting at the airport. Leaves this afternoon."

"When?" Lisa's voice rose an octave. She looked longingly at the Pacific Ocean. *Tell me I'm not hearing this.* "Come on, Francie. I finally make it to the coast just in time for the migration of the whales, and you send me off to cover a bed-and-breakfast?" She shouldn't complain. A job was a job, even a temporary assignment.

"What's wrong? Did you finally meet someone to take your mind off of Dale?"

"That's not it at all. He did me a favor by leaving. I was just hoping to see the sights while I was here this time. I've been going full speed for months. Give me a couple of days." She hoped her hard work would pay off soon. Lisa had bailed the magazine out of more binds this past year than she had had dates.

"Sorry to tell you this, dear, but we really need you to get moving on this right away."

Lisa moved the phone to the other ear as the editor explained the circumstances. One of these days, she would be able to be picky. Until then… "Of course I'll cover the story. I hope everything goes okay for the Greens and their baby."

"This place is north of Denver somewhere. Let me see here…Loveland. Hmm. Loveland—Valentine's Day. There's your angle. Get it?"

"I get it. And I'm familiar with the area. My sisters live—"

Her no-nonsense editor's voice broke her off. "Pull this one off, Lisa, and Steve's agreed to put you on the payroll full-time."

Those magical words caught her attention, even though she knew better than to get her hopes up. "Promises, promises," she said. "You know as well as I do Steve's been stringing me along for months."

"He's serious this time.…"

She paused, barely allowing Francie enough time

to finish her explanation. "I'm already interested," she said impatiently. "I didn't say no, did I?"

Lisa jotted down the airline and flight information. "E-mail me the specifics. I'll be in touch." She pressed End and set the phone in her bag.

Lisa glanced at her watch. "Francie, how could you do this to me again!" She had less than three hours to get to the airport, return the rental car and pick up her ticket. Lisa quickly reviewed the route on her map and took one last longing look at the waves hitting the jagged shore. *Footloose and fancy-free. I knew it would catch up with me. Farewell, San Francisco. Another time.*

The cash machine at the airport was out of money, ticket lines were frustratingly long and breakfast had worn off hours ago. Lisa slipped her boarding pass into her pack and ran down the concourse, her camera case bouncing along on built-in wheels.

When she reached the gate, the door was closed. Looking out the window, she saw her suitcase tossed into the luggage compartment beneath the airplane. She ran to the next desk and asked the agent for help. Moments later, a flight attendant met her at the end of the walk. "That was close," she said cheerfully. "We're just starting our preflight check."

"This flight does go to Denver, right?" Lisa asked breathlessly.

"Certainly does." The attendant read the row and

seat number. "Take your seat quickly, please, Ms. Berthoff. We'll be taking off momentarily."

"Sorry, I'm not usually so late." Lisa secured the pack on her shoulder. "My editor called just as I was headed to the Monterey Peninsula. So much for shooting the whales this year."

The woman's eyes opened wide. "Shoot?"

Lisa laughed. "I'm a photojournalist." She braced her camera case on her hip to squeeze through the aisle. "Only damage this thing can do is if it lands on someone."

The woman laughed. "I see. Have a nice flight." She opened an overhead compartment and helped secure Lisa's bag.

"Thank you." Lisa clicked her seat belt just before the plane backed away from the terminal. She leaned her head back, determined to relax.

As soon as the captain gave the clearance, Lisa used her laptop computer and checked for messages, hoping to find out transportation arrangements from Denver International Airport to the bed-and-breakfast. She would call Katarina and Emily once she knew more about her schedule. Raking the unruly strands of hair out of her eyes, Lisa took a deep breath. Come on, Francie.

Despite the frustrations of the sudden change in plans, she couldn't deny it would be good to see her older sisters again.

She knew Loveland was close to Springville, but she wasn't exactly sure where this bed-and-breakfast was in relation. Surely she could squeeze in a few days with Katarina and Emily before she rushed off on her next assignment. A smile teased her lips. Kevin and Emily's daughter would have her first birthday soon, while Katarina and Alex were due to have their first baby in just a few months. It seemed like just yesterday that she'd flown into a Colorado blizzard for their wedding. Had it really been a year already?

Memories invaded her thoughts and threatened to send her into a tailspin of emotions. She forced them away and moved to the next e-mail, making notes to send a requested article as soon as she reached the bed-and-breakfast. The Internet age had certainly simplified her job.

Francie's message finally arrived, instructing Lisa to take a shuttle to Loveland and wait for the proprietor.

"We received the attached brochure from the owner's sister. From what she sent us about the place, I think we might want to feature Whispering Pines Guest Ranch in our monthly column, 'America's Most Romantic Getaways.'"

Most romantic getaway? "You've got to be kidding," she muttered. Lisa turned off the laptop and put it away. How do I get stuck with these assignments? No one will take me seriously with stories like this. The passenger beside her left his seat and Lisa stretched her arms. "It's amazing what a person will do to get a job."

Several hours later, after taking a shuttle bus from Denver to Loveland, Lisa dragged her luggage to the curb.

A spry, silver-haired woman approached. "You must be ours." A smile crinkled her delicate pink skin and brought a sparkle to her eyes. "I'm Meg, from the ranch. We're so delighted that you're here."

She eyed Meg again. This frail-looking woman couldn't possibly run a ranch. "Are you sure? I mean, that you're expecting *me?*"

Meg snatched the huge suitcase from Lisa's grasp and hoisted it over the side of the truck. "Well, I did think there would be two of you," she said, glancing at the shuttle as it pulled away. "But if you're from the magazine, then this is just perfect."

Lisa nodded, suddenly a bit flustered. "I'm the Greens' replacement, Lisa Berthoff. The couple you were expecting went into premature labor."

"Oh, my. Well, I'm delighted that you're here, Lisa. Millie apologizes for not being able to pick you up herself."

Meg filled the thirty-minute drive with a history lesson on Whispering Pines Guest Ranch. "Millie has turned the ranch over to her son now."

Lisa learned that Meg and her late husband had worked for the Carter family for three decades. From Meg's descriptions, Lisa had wonderful mental pictures of the ranch, as well as the generous family determined to share their land with others instead of breaking it up into exclusive residential property.

Meg slowed the truck around a curve. The road opened before them into an enormous valley of gently rolling hills, jagged bluffs and wooded fringes. "Welcome to Whispering Pines Lodge, Adam's plan to save his grandparents' property," she said softly. "Bless his heart. He's put everything he has into saving this place."

"He must love it." Lisa pulled her camera from the bag and focused on the stately new guest house. "Wow…" She sighed. "Can you stop here, Meg? I want my first impressions on film."

Lisa hopped from the truck. The camera whirred.

On one side of the valley she photographed horses corralled between a weathered barn and split-rail fence. On the other, snow-dusted pine trees climbed the mountain. She snapped a series of shots of the icy creek meandering under a rustic stone bridge that separated a smaller home from the land where the new addition was located.

Lisa lowered the camera and filled her lungs with the pine scent. She paused. An odd feeling stirred within her. Anticipation was to be expected on any new job, but that wasn't all.

Mystified by the intensity she felt about this assignment as they drove closer to the lodge, Lisa felt her usually "on-edge" nerves dissipate. She squirmed in her seat, uneasy with the sense of hope and tranquillity. If she didn't know better, she'd think there was something to this romantic getaway idea.

How Meg had managed to convince a skeptic like

Lisa was a mystery. She'd given up on romance long ago. Yet, in that brief moment when she first saw Whispering Pines, it was as if she knew everything she needed to know in order to write this story.

Meg pulled through the circular drive to the impressive front entrance and shut off the engine. Lisa slid from the seat of the truck and looked around. In the distance a man carrying a huge ax over his shoulder like Paul Bunyan disappeared behind a miniature barn-shaped building.

Lisa lifted her eyebrows. Hmm, this may not be so bad after all. When he appeared again, Lisa was waiting with camera focused. Click...click...click... He propped the ax against a tall evergreen and turned toward her. The man was tall, broad-shouldered and much younger than she'd anticipated. He sauntered closer in long, purposeful strides. The lens cap dangled in the icy breeze, tapping against her hand.

Seconds later the man's hand pulled the camera away from her face.

"What are you doing?" Lisa yanked it from his hand and snapped the lens cover in place to protect it from any chance of damage. "Excuse me, but this is my camera."

"And this is my land." His voice left no room for discussion.

Lisa glanced up again. He had a strong jaw, deep-set eyes and sun bleached brown hair that desperately needed a cut. Nevertheless, he was still one drop-dead handsome cowboy. He crossed his arms over his chest and Lisa felt her heart race. Whispering Pines Guest Ranch. It couldn't be. "Adam?" She stepped back, confused. "I thought…"

He looked puzzled. He obviously didn't recognize her from their sisters' and brothers' weddings.

"I beg your pardon, ma'am. I don't believe we've met. May I ask what in tarnation you're doing with that camera?"

Pulling herself together, Lisa extended her hand. This was a professional assignment. Not a family gathering. The backpack slid from her shoulder, and with the flick of his wrist, the stunning proprietor caught it. Lisa lifted it back to her shoulder. "I'm taking pictures.…"

"I figured that much out." His frown deepened. "Question is, why?"

"I'm…" Momentarily, she wasn't sure who she was, and less sure of *what* she was doing here. "I'm Lisa Berthoff, Katarina and Emily's sister."

One eyebrow lifted. "Lisa?" A look of shock plastered onto his face, Adam tried to regain his composure. "I didn't recognize you."

No kidding. "Must be my hair. It was shorter."

"And…" Adam raised his hands to his hair and awkwardly let them drop again. "Umm…curlier."

Lisa nodded, remembering. "Yes, it was." The expense of curling her stubbornly straight hair was a luxury she'd had to go without after the surprise that awaited her return from Kat's wedding. The changes in her appearance were obviously not improvements from the look on Adam's face. She had stress to thank for the weight loss. Stress and Dale. Or were the two one and the same? At least her perception had improved since he'd walked out on her. When it came to men, she now had twenty-twenty vision. She'd been blinded by love once, but never again.

Adam stared, speechless.

Mrs. MacIntyre came down the guest house steps and broke the uncomfortable silence. "Lisa? I didn't know you were coming."

"Hello, Mrs. MacIntyre. The magazine sent me as a last-minute replacement for the Greens. I'm here to do the write-up on Adam…I mean, on Whispering Pines."

"Magazine? What magazine?" Adam said.

Ignoring his questions, his mother continued. "Call me Millie, please." She wrapped an arm around Lisa and looked at her son. "Isn't this just perfect, Adam, dear? Lisa's doing your story." Millie beamed, and her voice was overly enthusiastic, even by Lisa's estimation. "I can't wait to tell Elizabeth that you're here."

Adam plastered a smile across his face. "Is that so?" Without another word to her, Adam reached for Lisa's bags in the back of the truck. "Thanks for bringing our guest out, Meg. Have a good weekend."

"It was my pleasure. Enjoy your stay, Lisa."

"Thank you, Meg. I'm sure it will be wonderful."

Adam groaned, but whether it was because of the conversation or the seventy-pound suitcase he was lifting, Lisa wasn't sure. What did he expect? Her entire life was in these bags.

Adam glanced at his mother, who'd followed Meg to the white sedan in the parking lot across the yard. He turned to Lisa and lowered his voice. "And just to set things straight, Mrs.— Sorry, I didn't catch your married name."

Lisa was stunned. Married? What, or who, had given Adam the impression she had married?

"Never mind. Just so you realize, I'm not interested in advertising in any magazine nor am I doing any interview for one."

Keep your cool, Lisa. You need this job. "Thanks for clarifying that. Good thing I'm not in advertising, then, isn't it? And just to clear up one more thing…" She hated to add to his problems, whatever they might be, but she believed in honesty. "I'm not married."

"Great. Just great," he said, then took off across the flagstone walk, mumbling.

Millie's voice startled Lisa. "Oh, dear. Look at the time." Adam's mom smiled at Lisa then climbed into the truck, calling sweetly to Adam as he closed the distance between himself and the front door of the house. "Don't count on me for dinner tonight. I'm having dinner with Mr. Miller. Why don't you catch Lisa up on all the family news?" She turned the key and revved the engine. "Don't pay any attention to his grumbling, Lisa. He'll be fine soon.

I'm sure of it. I'll look forward to visiting with you tomorrow.''

''That would be nice. I'll see you then.'' Adam's mother headed down the hill and across the quaint bridge to the small Victorian-style house tucked behind the winter-bare tree branches. Lisa let out a deep breath and straightened her shoulders. With a sigh of determination, she ran up the log steps, in search of the very handsome, impatient and presumably still-single bed-and-breakfast owner. She was going to set things straight, once and for all.

Chapter Two

Adam heard the door close downstairs, followed by a thump, then a muffled voice and...giggles? He dropped Lisa's luggage in the middle of the floor and ran out of the room.

He didn't have any doubt what had caused the calamity. His brother's idea of a bachelor's perfect birthday gift—a Newfoundland-mix puppy.

"To-by!" Taking the log stairs two at a time, Adam arrived at the front door to find Lisa flat on the ground with his overgrown puppy giving her kisses. Lisa's laughter did nothing more than encourage the dog. Adam grabbed Toby's collar and hauled the one-hundred-pound pup off her.

"Toby, *sit!*" Adam didn't take the time to lead the animal to a designated location; he just hoped Toby would sit somewhere and quit causing trouble. He extended his arm to help Lisa up, instantly reminding him of his unwelcome reaction to her delicate hand in his a few minutes earlier. "Are you okay?"

Accepting Adam's hand, Lisa jumped up off the floor and untwisted her camera strap. "I'm fine." With a soft chuckle, she wiped Toby's kisses from her cheek. "Now that's what I call a warm welcome."

Adam stepped back and released her hand. "Please accept my apology. I haven't had much time to train him."

"Looks like you're going to have your hands full." Brushing dirt. and dog hair off her black sweater and leggings, Lisa turned toward Toby, positioned her camera, clicked the shutter, then snapped the cover back onto the lens.

She looked different than she had at his oldest brother's wedding a year ago. And it was more than the chic hairstyle. He didn't remember Lisa being so thin. She was still as pretty, but something was definitely different. Still...how could he have not recognized her?

"Good thing I like dogs. Never had one of my own, but..." She smiled at Toby. "Who can resist falling in love with an adorable face like his?"

That was enough to set the dog in motion again, still trailing the remnants of his third leash, aka teething rope, behind him. Before Adam could stop Toby, he was on his hind legs and in her face again. This time, Adam sprang forward in time to catch Lisa.

With one arm firmly around her small waist, unwelcome feelings returned. Adam struggled to find his voice. "That's it, Toby. Outside!"

As Adam helped Lisa regain her footing, he felt his anger turn from the energetic dog toward Elizabeth for getting him into this mess.

He'd had no idea his sister was serious about advertising in a national magazine. Where did she think they were going to come up with that kind of money? And even if they had the money, why would he be willing to let anyone do any kind of a story on himself? Especially right now, with this deadline looming ahead of him. With the winter they'd had, he was now weeks behind schedule.

He stepped away to take the dog outside.

"Ouch!" Lisa fell backward against him. "Wait, my hair's caught on something."

Adam again offered his support while struggling to see what had happened. Lisa grabbed her hair and tugged, also yanking the button of his shirt.

"Hold on a minute," Adam said, steadying her. He gently fanned her hair, releasing a faint scent. He inhaled again. Trying to ignore how good she smelled and the feel of her silky hair, he untangled a few strands at a time.

He was used to the well-meaning grandmothers at the church trying to play matchmaker, but his own family? When had everyone decided he needed company out here? And how in the world had Elizabeth pulled off bringing his brothers' single sister-in-law here under the pretense of business?

He'd been suspicious when the unmarried interior decorator showed up to help with the lodge, but finally convinced himself it was a coincidence. Then when he figured out the Sweetheart Festival coordinator was also available, he began to smell a skunk. Now Lisa. He couldn't believe his own brothers and sisters would stoop to such levels.

He was obviously wrong.

Didn't much matter now. Faced with this awkward situation, Adam realized the first step was to get Lisa out of here before this got any more out of hand.

He couldn't deny that Lisa was a looker, from her bright blue eyes to her classy dismissal of his pet's poor behavior.

He instinctively smoothed her hair. "There, I think that's it."

Lisa turned around within the confines of his embrace, and for an instant, Adam forgot he wanted nothing to do with this woman who wanted to dig into his life.

She tipped her head back, her gaze meeting his, furthering the temptation to ignore exactly why she was here. Her cheeks turned a healthy pink. What am I thinking? She's family.

Her voice was gentle and soft, yet confident at the same time. "Thanks. If you wouldn't mind telling me where my room is, then you can get back to what you were doing before I arrived."

Her comment stopped him in his tracks. As if she knew what he was thinking, one corner of her mouth hinted at a smile. Before she came…what was I doing? Adam released her, content that Lisa and her beautiful smile were now safe from his puppy's affections.

And his.

This wasn't the time to tell the eager photojournalist she was wasting her time here. He'd tell her that later, over dinner. Once he'd calmed his nerves and collected his thoughts.

"Up the stairs, third door on the right. If you need anything, I'll be out back."

He reached out to help with her coat, an amazingly sensible choice for a sophisticated city girl.

"Thanks." She backed away, then turned and nearly tripped up the first step.

From the corner of his eye, he watched her climb the stairs, kicking himself for torturing himself so. He shook his head. I've got too many things to do as it is without an attractive woman to distract me. "Dinner will be ready at six sharp."

"Fine, I'll see you then," she said cheerfully.

When she was well out of earshot he muttered, "Everything *was* fine, before *you* showed up."

"Boy, that was telling him, Lisa. 'Set him straight once and for all,'" she mimicked her own words as she walked down the hall. "What's gotten into me?" She framed her warm face with her cool hands.

"Adam MacIntyre is no more than an assignment. An assignment I can't afford to botch."

Lisa turned into the third room on the right and found her luggage in the middle of the floor. She glanced at the window and forced herself to ignore the sound of Adam chopping wood. Without thinking, Lisa moved her clothes into the beautifully refurbished oak dresser and set a fresh outfit on the dusty blue plaid bedspread. The six-foot-high mission-style headboard matched the frame of the vanity mirror. A pair of armchairs and a table sat in front of the window.

The rhythmic sound outside was like a lariat around her, pulling her toward the bay window. She eased the coordinating tab-top curtains open, feeling like a teenager peeking at the boy next door. *I thought it was just the tux. I never dreamed Adam would be this handsome in everyday clothes.*

Toby was tied to a fence post, well out of danger from flying wood. And wood was flying. Each swing of Adam's ax went straight through to the stump below. He neatly stacked the split logs, then repeated the motions.

She recalled Adam's strong arms guarding her from the playful pup. His fingers gently untangling her stringy hair from the button of his shirt. She felt her cheeks flush again and forced away thoughts of romance. She was here to do a job. Nothing more.

Adam was the subject. She was the journalist. Oil and water. And the two did not mix. Lisa had learned that lesson long ago, along with a few others. There wasn't time to meet, let alone develop, any sort of meaningful relationship when your life was on the road.

That was what had drawn her to Dale. They were both wanderers—lured by adventure for nothing more than adventure's sake. They were a team. He was the photographer, she the journalist. Now she was both. Alone and on her own.

Which was just the way Lisa liked it. It was much less painful that way. She'd come too far in the past year to let anything or anyone slow her down. Especially not the last available MacIntyre brother. Nothing against her sisters' husbands, but she wasn't interested in making the *Guinness Book of World Records* for most sisters to marry into the same family.

Now she knew why they'd been so anxious for her to come visit. It had nothing to do with seeing them. They wanted to set her up with Adam. Nice try, gals.

Francie's words taunted. "Romantic Getaways. Loveland. Valentine's Day—get it?" Lisa again admired Adam. "Gullible and naive—that's me." How had Emily and Katarina managed to convince her editor to arrange this?

To Francie's credit, she had been there when Lisa was at her lowest. She'd been a friend when Lisa was trying to pick up the pieces of her life and struggling to find work. Francie didn't give up hope that the managing editor would find a place for Lisa on the staff. The woman was a dreamer. Lisa was a realist. It would never happen. But Lisa didn't care. She wasn't quite ready to forego traveling anyway.

Not even her sisters understood Lisa's career choice. Of all people, she'd thought they would understand.

Emily had broken her engagement to pursue her desire to become a doctor. Yet after eight years apart, Emily had her career, the man she'd left behind and two adorable children.

Katarina had turned down a lucrative business offer in order to keep her own dream alive. An answer to her prayer, according to Katarina. She had spent the past year expanding production of her exclusive doll designs. She was now happily married, CEO of a successful company and soon to be a new mother.

Yes, every dream has its price. Lisa's happened to mean constant traveling, digging up stories and hoping each assignment would be the one to open her own door to success. Opportunity rarely knocked more than once in this business. She had to be ready when that time came.

Lisa took a deep breath and gazed into the purple and fuchsia sky. In the distance she could see the very top of a sawlike ridge silhouetted against the fading sunset. All around, trees and red rock formations added to the allure of the remote ranch. Lisa didn't need to wonder what motivated Adam to stay here. Even in the middle of a dry winter, it was beautiful.

Secluded.

Peaceful.

Comforting.

Yes, a place like this could grow on a person—enough to bring one back after years in the city. She smiled at the immediate warmth she'd felt for Adam's mother. According to Meg, Millie Carter was lured away by love, and drawn home for the same reason. She'd grown up on this ranch, and it was no surprise that Whispering Pines had called her back.

Despite Millie's kindness, something his mother had done obviously wore Adam's patience thin. To Adam's defense, Lisa knew it had to be difficult to have a life of his own with his family living so near. Had he, too, been lured away from Whispering Pines for love? And what had brought him home?

Being the youngest child, she wondered if Adam hadn't yet cut the apron strings, or if he felt obligated to take care of his mother after his father's death. From personal experience, she knew how difficult that last child leaving home was on a mother, especially a single mother.

Her stomach growled and Lisa looked at her watch—5:40. She barely had time to freshen up. Adam had stopped chopping wood and was probably preparing supper, just daring her to be late.

Chapter Three

Lisa rushed through the great room in search of the kitchen, hoping Adam wouldn't notice the time. Following the distinct aroma of sautéed onions, she found him.

She paused silently to admire the damp-haired, barefoot cowboy again. Adam looked as much at ease in the kitchen as he had outside chopping wood. The navy blue T-shirt stretched across his powerful shoulders and the Levi's hugged his slim hips perfectly. Where's the camera when I need it?

"Evening. Beautiful sunset, wasn't it? Of course, probably doesn't compare to those you've seen." Without looking up, he knew she was there.

There was no hope of denying she'd been watching him, as he'd obviously seen her at the window and already made his own assumptions. "Yes, it was. When my editor called this morning, I wasn't very pleased that I had to miss a photo shoot of the Pacific, but tonight, I have no regrets. Colorado's sunsets are truly among the most beautiful in the nation.''

''A mover and a shaker. One day here, there the next,'' he snapped. ''If God had meant for such a frantic pace, He wouldn't have created such beautiful sights to be appreciated.''

Lisa didn't understand what had upset Adam, but she couldn't afford to let it continue—she needed this story. Lisa glanced again at her watch. She was only five minutes late. Surely that wasn't what he was mad about. Nevertheless she apologized.

''No problem.''

The lack of conversation echoed through the room as Adam worked, whisking the white sauce to a velvety smooth texture. He combined onions, white sauce, potatoes and chunks of soft cheese in silence.

''Can I help?''

He sprinkled seasonings into the pan and shook his head. ''It'll be ready in a minute.''

''Listen, Adam, I don't know what I've done to trouble you. I'm here to do a job, which I hope ends up helping you as well as myself. Is there a problem?''

He set two soup mugs by the stove. ''Liz suggested advertising in a national magazine. I didn't approve of the idea then, and to be honest, I still don't.''

Perplexed, Lisa shook her head and leaned against

the counter across from him. "Why don't we start at the beginning? First of all, this isn't an advertisement, it's an article. Secondly, I received an assignment this morning which called me away from the beauty of the Pacific Ocean—migrating whales, white-capped waves, deep blue water." She paused, realizing her sisters couldn't have had anything to do with her coming here. "I left a personal trip to do this article, and you're telling me you don't know a thing about it? Nor do you want it done at all?" She crossed her arms over her chest.

His remorseful gaze met hers and she was struck with a sudden unexpected longing to make Adam understand how important this was to her. In her life, this was more than just another stop. It was a chance to start over. In Adam's, it was a major interruption to the peace and quiet he took for granted.

"I'm sorry, Lisa. I'm sure there's something more important for you to cover than a small-town guest ranch's grand opening." He looked away. "Truth is, it's not a good time. As you can see, this place is nowhere near ready for a celebration, let alone impressive enough for national exposure."

Lisa looked at the empty diagonal wood-plank walls, the bare windows, the kitchen cabinets waiting for knobs. "We don't have to focus on the kitchen. My suite looked beautiful. Coordinating towels and bedding, gorgeous antiques—"

"Your room is the only one finished," he interrupted. "Apparently my mother was expecting you."

Was she imagining the emphasis he'd put on the word *you?* Was he upset that she was assigned to the story? "No, Adam, your mother may have been expecting the Greens, but I didn't even know I was coming until this morning," Lisa insisted. "And I had no clue it was to your ranch." She leaned over the counter and sniffed the homemade soup. Her eyes drifted closed with contentment. "The timing couldn't be more perfect. What could be more romantic than a February grand opening in Loveland, Colorado?"

"Romantic? Who said anything about romance?" Adam ripped open a pouch of saltines and dumped them into a small basket, then chopped through the chunk of cheese as if it, too, had done something wrong. "What magazine are you with, anyway?"

"I'm a freelancer. I don't work for anyone exclusively." Why did that sound so much more impressive than it was in reality? "This is for a bed-and-breakfast magazine."

"Number one...I own a guest ranch, not a B and B."

"That's okay. The column is on romantic getaways. There's no need to refer to bed-and-breakfast."

"Number two...it's not a romantic getaway. It's a guest ranch. You know, horses, cows, rustic." Adam pulled a stainless-steel ladle from the hook over the stove and filled the two mugs. "I hope you like potato soup. It's my specialty."

Not exactly welcoming, but it was most likely as close as she would get right now. "You're in luck. I love it. How can I help?"

After an obvious pause, Adam said, "Glasses are in that cupboard. I'll take water, but there's also milk and iced tea in the refrigerator if you'd prefer." He picked up the small cutting board with the cheese on it and headed through the alcove. "We'll eat in the dining room." Adam disappeared and an instant later, light filtered through the doorway.

Lisa filled the glasses and set the drinks on the table. Adam carried baskets of crackers and rolls in one hand and the plates in the other. In a few minutes, Lisa and Adam were seated at the smallest table in the sparsely furnished room. Adam said a prayer, then jumped up and turned the lights brighter. She smiled inside. It didn't matter to her, in either dim light or bright, Adam was the epitome of "tall, dark and handsome" and looked nothing like his fair-haired brothers.

Adam became increasingly quiet.

Lisa took a spoonful of the thick soup, trying to erase her rampant thoughts. This was a business trip, not some romantic escape, and the best way to convince him of that would be to stick to the assignment. "So, tell me what you want this article to say about Whispering Pines."

He stared into his soup as he crumbled the saltines over the top. "Which part of 'no' do you not understand?"

She set down her spoon and looked Adam in the eye. "I hear it. I just don't believe it. We're talking national exposure, Adam. Do you realize the magnitude of that?"

He leaned back in his chair, a puzzled look on his face. "Maybe I'm hearing and not quite believing it, Lisa. The family was sitting around one night after working on the landscaping, trying to come up with ideas to promote the place." He paused, as if thinking through the conversation. "I'd been knee-deep in renovations and worrying about the balloon payment on the construction loan. Advertising was out of the question. Especially in a national magazine. Elizabeth mentioned some contest..."

"That was for the most romantic getaway, but the actual contest is over. It was so popular they've decided to make America's Most Romantic Getaways a monthly feature. Actually, I believe this will be in the bridal issue."

"The *what?*" His jaw fell open. He dropped his fist on the table, clanging the dishes. Adam rambled on as if this were the end of the world. "Besides, who'd have thought a half-built lodge would get any attention?" He shook his head and rolled his eyes. "She didn't mention it again, and I thought the subject was dead."

Lisa laughed, ignoring his scowl. "In a town named Loveland? Who'd have ever imagined? You should put her in charge of your PR, if you haven't already."

"Thanks, but no thanks. I have enough trouble keeping my sisters at bay lately. I don't want the publicity—especially not as some romantic getaway."

Panic coursed through her. "What better way to bring in business than with free exposure?" She paused. "The only thing this costs you is putting up with me for a few days. And if that's a problem, I'm sure my sisters wouldn't mind company."

"That's not a problem, though I'm sure your sisters would love to see you. I'm sorry I've made you feel unwelcome, but I don't think I can be of much help with your story right now." Adam took another bite. "Maybe you could come back in the summer?"

"I can mention that to my editor, but I don't think they'll go for it…to be quite honest." Lisa watched his strong hand lift the comparably tiny spoon to his mouth, picturing herself behind the camera, capturing every nuance of this man's character.

Where God closes a door, he opens a window. Her optimistic sister's words slapped her in the ego—again. In your life, maybe, but not mine.

Adam cleared his throat. "Mom mentioned some couple coming for the week, but I never thought…" He'd never in his wildest dreams imagined Lisa would spend a week at his ranch. As strong as the attraction had been a year ago, he'd managed to keep a tight rein on his emotions. She'd been seeing someone at the time, and he'd had a huge project to complete. In the thirteen months since Alex and Katarina's wedding, not a word had been said about that ridiculous bouquet, or getting the two of them together.

Still, he couldn't just kick Lisa off the ranch. No matter how badly he wanted to. She was practically a relative.

As if she read his mind, she became silent. The twinkle in her bright blue eyes disappeared. "I'm sure you've had a very long day, Adam. Why don't we put the article aside for tonight?" She took a spoonful of soup and a slice of cheese. "Tell me what you've been up to since the wedding."

Lisa had emptied her bowl by the time he'd quit talking about the vast construction project. Despite the fact that he'd deliberately made the year sound as mundane as possible, a sparkle of admiration returned. Eyes like hers could make a weak man sell his soul to the tabloids without one regret.

"So, you're a talented craftsman, an industrious businessman and a great cook, too. The soup was delicious."

"Thanks. Would you like more?" Adam pushed his chair away from the antique oak table, anxious to put some space between them.

"I'd love some, thanks. Where'd you learn to cook?" She stood and walked into the kitchen with him.

Adam watched her refill her soup mug, noting similarities between Lisa and each of her sisters. Like Emily, she hadn't let her underprivileged childhood keep her from dreaming. And like Katarina, Lisa overflowed with enthusiasm and creativity. He'd seen her work in several magazines.

He tore his gaze from her as she disappeared into the dining room, recalling her question. Realizing that every word he said played right into her hand, he held back. "My dad liked to cook. I guess I got it from him."

"Oh? Do Kevin and Alex cook, too?" she asked as she pecked around the corner, her eyes wide with curiosity.

And like both sisters, she was what any man would consider attractive. Adam wondered about her life, constantly on the move. "Alex does. Kevin can't boil water." Turning the conversation around, he asked, "You still living out of a suitcase, or have you found a place to call home? Between assignments, that is."

"I've been too busy to settle down."

Did he detect a note of sadness in her remark? "I guess that's good in your business, right?"

She hesitated. "I can't complain. It pays the bills." Lisa took another spoonful of soup.

He nodded. "Don't you ever miss going home? Sinking into your own bed? Eating a home-cooked meal?"

She looked at him as if he were speaking a foreign language. Or at the very least, as if he'd asked her to spill some deep dark secret.

Lisa held up the soup mug. "I am eating a home-cooked meal. I'm in a beautiful home, and the company isn't bad, either.'' Her pink lips turned up stiffly at the corners. ''Don't you ever long to see all those wonderful sights to be appreciated out in this vast world?'' Her voice softened. ''Don't you wonder if you're in the right place, doing the right thing?'' It cracked. ''Don't you ever just want to take off and avoid all this responsibility?''

Now it was his turn to look at her as if she were from another world. He couldn't believe the regret he felt, exposing the pain he heard in her soft voice. ''My roots are in this soil, and I'll do everything it takes to keep them planted right here. The last thing I want is to disrupt the peace with chaos of the outside world. I thank God every day for taking me out of the corporate world and bringing me home.''

''How nice.'' She stood up, cleared her place and took her dishes to the kitchen.

Her icy response instantly made him recall Kat and Emily's concern about their little sister's hurried life and Lisa's distance from God. He winced. This wasn't going well at all.

''Adam, it's been a very long day. I think I'll call it a night.''

''I didn't mean to say anything to offend you, Lisa.'' He wanted to reach out to her, to take his words back, or at the very least, have the chance to ease their discomfort. ''I promise it won't—''

Without turning around, she said, ''Don't bother, Adam. Promises mean nothing to me. I'll see you in the morning.''

Chapter Four

Adam locked the front door, ready to put the day behind him. He needed sleep. It looked as if tomorrow would be another long day.

He turned around, greeted by the coat rack. Lisa's coat instantly reminded him of how nice she had felt in his embrace. She was tempting as homemade apple pie—a perfect mixture of sweet and tart.

What was he thinking? He hadn't as much as been on an official date in three years. And if he planned to see someone, a woman who spent her life on the road would not be the one for him.

Lisa had a portfolio full of dreams, and enough talent to make them come true. Despite the challenges of her early years, she, like her sisters, had stomped on the restrictions their meager background could have inflicted on them. Each one had set goals and never gave up until she reached them.

Adam closed the door between the lodge and his private quarters, the modest ranch house his grand-parents had built in the early forties. Climbing the narrow stairs to the attic bedroom, Adam found it odd to think he had his first guest staying in his new lodge. Even more perplexing that it was Lisa.

He spent half the night awake, wondering how to protect his heart from the unwelcome woman at the tip of Cupid's arrow. Despite recent efforts by many well-meaning friends and relatives, no woman had caught his eye since Alex and Katarina's wedding. He and Lisa had spent the better part of the blizzard sipping hot chocolate and telling stories about their brothers and sisters. He immediately discovered Lisa wasn't an easy woman to get to know. She didn't like talking about herself, her accomplishments or her feelings.

Why the drifter had made such an impression on him, he wasn't sure. It was more than her looks, as there were plenty of good-looking women in his life. With each tidbit he picked up about the youngest Berthoff sister from his brothers, Adam realized he stood a better chance of surviving a stampede than he did falling in love with Lisa. She wasn't his type. Wanderlust was in her blood, and he was more than content in his own corner of the world.

Lisa was a journalist. Her job came first. After all, that's why she was here. She hadn't come to see him, or even her sisters. It was a story she was after. A story about a romantic getaway. That means big trouble for the ranch, and me.

It had taken him long enough to find where he belonged, and he'd be sure that no one—especially not a woman with no ties to family or land—came between him and the dreams God had called him home to.

Adam didn't need or want his life turned inside out by a stubborn woman who didn't believe in promises, or God, or slowing down long enough to see exactly what she was missing. A loner like himself had no business tying anyone else down to his obligations.

Keeping Lisa around in the confines of his lodge was definitely asking for trouble. Regardless of her familial connections or her charming personality, the beautiful drifter couldn't stay. Wouldn't, even if he'd be foolish enough to ask her to.

While he wouldn't exactly call his ranch secluded, it was a far cry from the hub of activity Lisa was accustomed to. Just yesterday, she had started her day with plans of whale-watching, and by the end of the day she was in Colorado to write a totally different story on a bed-and-breakfast. The world was her playground, and this ranch was his world.

While his brothers had followed in their father's footsteps of the construction business, Adam had counted the years, just waiting for the day his parents would let him spend summers helping his grandparents run the ranch. Now he had that chance. Whispering Pines was all he had to remember his grandparents by and he would do everything within his power to maintain the legacy they had left behind.

This was his dream. His destiny. His calling. And if he couldn't make a go of the guest ranch, his cousin would be more than happy to put his own name on the deed. Chance had offered to buy the MacIntyre cousins out in the very beginning, and still did on a regular basis. At the going price of land in the area, and the rate of population growth, they all knew their opportunistic cousin probably had investors lined up to divide and develop the entire ranch.

Lisa's mission stirred up fears and shadows, from the list of unfinished detail work, to decorating the place, to the warning that mixing business and romance was a lethal combination. While it helped that he knew Lisa's family, trusting *any* woman with his business image would always bring back caustic memories of all that Amelia's betrayal had cost him.

As usual, all it took was one inkling of a reminder of that dark time in his life to ruin the entire night's rest. He tossed and turned, barely catching a wink of sleep before he heard the alarm clock's dutiful "cock-a-doodle-doo." Back to work.

Adam stepped into the house a few hours later, followed by a chilling gust of wind. To his surprise, Lisa was sitting by the window enjoying a cup of coffee, reading the morning newspaper, seemingly oblivious to the vehicles driving up the lane. "You think the entire family can convince me to go along with this?''

Minutes earlier Adam had seen Kevin's SUV pull through the Whispering Pines gate, followed by Alex's truck. If his brothers were coming to work, they'd have driven out in one vehicle, which meant this was a family visit, not business.

She looked up from the paper. ''Good morning to you, too. Now what have I done?''

Without a word, Adam pointed out the window. ''Face it. This idea of my sister's backfired. End of subject. You may as well take your matching set of luggage and head on down the road to the next golden opportunity.'' He pulled a mug from the cupboard and poured a cup of coffee.

''You're even crankier than usual this morning. Didn't you sleep well? I suppose that's my fault, too.'' Lisa took a sip of coffee and turned back to her newspaper.

As a matter of fact, it is.

She glanced out the window, then stood up and placed her hands on her hips. ''Adam, I *didn't* call anyone. I wasn't sure I'd even be here long enough.''

''You're right about that.'' He lifted the mug to his mouth. ''You'd like me to believe the whole family just happened to show up out of the blue on a Saturday morning?'' Without thinking, he took a drink.

''That's hot. Be—'' she winced ''—careful.''

He spit the coffee back into the mug before he realized what he was doing. "Phew."

He set the mug on the counter and opened the freezer. He dropped two ice cubes into the steaming brew. "I should have known. I wasn't paying attention to what I was doing, I guess." From the feel of his burned tongue, it would be a long while before he'd make the same mistake.

"Believe what you want about my sisters, Adam. I had nothing to do with it." She shook her head. "I don't know why they're here, but I can't think of a better way to prove my innocence to someone as...as...bullheaded as you."

He walked closer with quick, long, purposeful strides. Adam cocked his head questioningly. "Bullheaded? You sure you don't want to add *cad* to that? If my memory serves me correctly, that was the word of choice at the church after Kat and Alex's wedding. You sure you don't want to come up with a few more names for me?" The words slipped from his mouth before he thought about the implication, that he'd been thinking of that darned bouquet.

Lisa folded the newspaper and neatly put it back into the copper boiler next to the small Franklin stove heating the kitchen. "I think that will do fine for now. Given time, I'm sure I could come up with a few more that fit your sour disposition."

Thankful that she hadn't seemed to catch his slip, Adam returned to the entry. He slid the heel of his cowboy boot into the wooden boot jack and tugged first one foot, then the other from the fitted leather.

"It's no wonder you're still an eligible bachelor if you're always this charming," she muttered.

"I heard that, and I couldn't be happier." Adam stood at the doorway to the great room and waited. "Must be all that running that makes you so miserable."

Car doors slammed on the opposite side of the lodge, and Adam returned to the coffeemaker, pausing long enough to add a spot of hot coffee to the overly cooled liquid. "Come on." He nodded his head toward the front door.

"Whatever makes you think I'm miserable?" Lisa's feet were planted to the oak floor, her arms crossed.

"Later. Right now, we have bigger fish to fry. And you're not getting out of this one." Adam caught her by the elbow and firmly escorted her to the front oom to wait for their guests.

Lisa pulled her arm from his grip. "What has you so worried, Adam? This story...?" Lisa sank into the leather sofa with her back to the door and stared defiantly at him. "Or did you tell someone that we caught that bouquet? I thought that was *our* secret."

He set his cup of coffee down on the marble coffee table with a crash, spilling hot liquid on his hand. He muttered under his breath. "I didn't tell a soul. As for the story, Liz sent the paperwork, I didn't. This is a bad time, is all."

Lisa crossed her arms over her chest.

His voice faltered and he narrowed his eyes in warning. "Don't look at me that way." He pulled a couple of tissues from the box on the mantel and wiped up the spilled coffee, then tossed them into a wicker trash can as the doorbell rang.

"Yoo-hoo! Adam? Anyone home?"

Despite his chilling glare, Lisa kept her back to the door and remained silent.

He was minimally surprised that she didn't back down. Not that he should be. After all, he'd heard stories from his brothers of how stubborn her sisters were. Why should this Berthoff woman be any different?

Adam glanced at the houseguest, then to her sisters, who didn't seem to notice Lisa sitting on his sofa. He was surprised to see Susan and Elizabeth had also arrived while he and Lisa were arguing.

"What's the big emergency?" Alex asked as he helped the very pregnant Katarina take her coat off.

"Emergency?" Adam echoed.

Kevin took Alissa from her car seat while Emily showed Ricky where to put his wet snow boots.

After a quick "Hi, Uncle Adam," Susan's boys grabbed hold of Ricky and ran directly to the private family room to play with Adam's stash of old toys. "Mom called and said we all needed to be here in an hour. What's so important that you had to wake us all at the crack of dawn on a Saturday morning?"

Susan, Elizabeth and their husbands shared their annoyance at the early beckon to rush right over.

The door opened once more, and Millie strolled inside with a smile on her face. "Morning, everyone. How about some warm muffins fresh out of the oven?"

The room hushed to an eerie silence.

All eyes were on Adam. He raised his hands in front of him. "Don't look at me. This isn't my doing."

Lisa stood and turned around, diverting the attention away from him. "Hi, everyone." Her bright clear blue eyes gleamed with satisfaction.

Lisa's sisters screamed as they made their way over to greet their youngest sister. Emily hugged Lisa and held her at arm's length. "I didn't even recognize you. You're so thin...."

Katarina nudged Emily aside and took her turn for a hug. "You look wonderful, Lisa. What are you doing here? Why didn't you call?"

Alex glanced at Adam with a puzzled look, and Kevin, still holding his curly-haired toddler, gave Adam the thumbs-up, then took his daughter over to meet her long-lost aunt. The toddler immediately grabbed a handful of Lisa's silky blond hair.

Adam caught Susan shrugging her shoulders as Elizabeth asked why they'd been called over for a Berthoff family reunion.

"Lisa, why didn't you tell us you were coming?" Emily's smile and question were genuine.

"I didn't know. It was a last-minute assignment. I just arrived last night." Lisa smiled at the child, seemingly wary of frightening the child. "I meant to call. I just ran out of time." Her voice was soft, and she covered her eyes, playing peekaboo with Alissa. The toddler giggled, then hid her face in the crook of Emily's neck.

He had no more doubts that Lisa was right. This time his paranoia was getting the best of him. Too much time spent trying to avoid Cupid's arrow, he guessed. The fact that the festival coordinator had managed to dub Adam and herself as host and hostess for the masquerade probably didn't help right now.

With their niece in her arms, Lisa made her way through the crowd to him. "Now are you convinced?"

"Point made," he grumbled, giving Alissa a raspberry on her baby-soft neck. The toddler instantly dove into his waiting hands. "It still doesn't mean I want to be a part of your magazine."

Elizabeth's eyes lit up. "The magazine? You mean, we—we're going to be featured? Really?"

Lisa's eyes brimmed with mischief. "Not if your brother doesn't stop being so obstinate."

Adam felt his face turning red. "I never dreamed you were serious, Liz. You might have warned me. Who would have thought an unfinished lodge would stand a chance? Especially as a *romantic* bed-and-breakfast."

Elizabeth winced at her brother's raised voice. "You've opened Grandma and Grandpa's house to others as if it were a bed-and-breakfast since the day you moved in, Adam. If adding a touch of romance can help us keep the ranch in the family, isn't it worth considering?"

"Not only does my brochure not mention bed-and-breakfast *or* romance, but we're not even open yet. Didn't you have to send testimonials or something?"

While the others laughed, Elizabeth immediately defended herself. "I sent your brochure as is without one change. Remember, romance is a matter of personal opinion. As for customer recommendation, you shouldn't be surprised that your friends gave you wonderful reviews. Admit it, Adam, this was a great idea."

He had to remember, though he held the majority of the interest in Whispering Pines, he couldn't forget that he wouldn't be standing in this spacious guest house without the help of his family. Kevin and Alex had donated their time and talent on the lodge construction, Elizabeth and her husband, Kirk, had offered not only financial backing, but business insight, as well. Susan and Mike had donated manual labor to the project each weekend. And without his mother's encouragement, Adam never would have had the courage to tackle the project at all.

"Why don't we have some muffins and juice?" Millie suggested. "I see Adam has coffee made."

The conversation eventually drifted away from the

article, but not before Liz made arrangements to come back later in the day to visit with Lisa and show her around the ranch. After serving refreshments, Adam's mom and sisters left, leaving only Lisa's family.

While the women visited, Adam, Alex and Kevin discussed unfinished details on the lodge. When they returned, Emily and Katarina had already bundled the little ones in their coats and were ready to leave. "We'll see you both at church in the morning, right?"

Adam looked directly at Lisa, waiting for her response. "Your sister's welcome to join us."

Before Lisa could reply, Katarina waddled over to give Adam a hug. "It's settled, then. Sunday dinner will be at our house this week. Emily's on call."

Lisa took her coat from the hook and followed them out the door. He watched her hug everyone goodbye, then walk around the side of the lodge with Toby.

Standing alone in the foyer, Adam said, "I'd sure like to know how you worked this one out, Lord."

Chapter Five

When Lisa returned to the lodge after saying good-bye to her sisters and playing with Toby, the huge log house was empty. Adam had cleaned up and disappeared.

Without Adam to distract her, she had the chance to study the lodge and understand Adam's claim that there was a lot to be done before the grand opening. There was a lot of potential. Had Adam hired a decorator to add those final touches, or did he have a girlfriend who was going to help?

The mantel clock chimed. Elizabeth wouldn't be back for another hour.

She wondered if Adam had taken pictures of the entire process from beginning to finish, and retrieved her camera. She started upstairs in the guest suites. As Adam had claimed, none of the other rooms were ready for guests.

Antique furniture stood against bare walls, gathered by color and style. Furnishings for the two-bedroom suites were all rustic mission-style, like in her own suite. One furniture set included a matching marble-top dresser and washstand, yet another was a massive darker collection with a bed so high off the ground, she would need a step stool to climb in. On the far side such a stool stood next to the bed frame. All looked as if they had been refinished recently and were beautifully matched.

Pillow-top mattresses and goose-down pillows still wore their plastic coverings and Do Not Remove Under Penalty Of The Law tags. On each antique table or desk was a compact disc player/radio/clock still in the box. On one library table stood a dozen lamps, some old, some new, some matching and many unique designs.

Windows were stark frames to the beautiful backdrop of Colorado scenery. Ceiling fans waited anxiously for the summer heat.

Each bathroom was different. Some had oversize walk-in showers, while others replica clawfoot tubs, and pedestal sinks. The largest suite had a double-size jetted tub.

She snapped photos, hoping Adam wouldn't mind. They weren't for professional purposes, but for him, just for fun. This had to have been a huge undertaking to oversee the design, plans, purchases and building. She could see now why the cowboy was stressed.

Lisa finished the roll of film in the great room and kitchen, again, enthralled with the impressive collection of antiques—Hoosier cupboards, iceboxes of varied sizes and one intriguing massive oak chest with a dozen shallow drawers and at least another half-dozen cupboards, not counting the hidden compartments on each side of the unit.

By the time Liz returned from her mother's house, Lisa was armed with questions. She heard the back door open and close.

"Lisa?"

"In here." Lisa paused, studying the collection of compact discs and books in the Ballister bookshelf and the computer-generated note inviting guests to enjoy the discs in their rooms. "Quite a collection."

Adam's sister smiled. "We all made contributions, along with donations from friends who'd received a few rather interesting titles from club memberships."

"Ah, that explains it." She laughed. "It looks like you should have something to please everyone."

"That's Adam's goal." Elizabeth curled up on the leather sofa and invited Lisa to do the same. "You may have noticed, he's a little tense right now. He's not normally so crabby."

"I'm sorry to have come at a bad time. Who did my editor call to make the arrangements? It really isn't like Francie to push for an interview. It's not like this is breaking news. Whispering Pines will still be here in a month or two."

Elizabeth's smile softened. "Mom took the call.

She hoped it would give Adam a push to accept some help with the final details, like purchasing the linens, the bedding, the window coverings. He fired the decorator and doesn't want to accept help from Mom, Susan or I."

Lisa couldn't hide her surprise. "And when is the opening?"

"In three weeks." His sister jumped from the sofa, made a selection from the CDs and put one into the sound system.

Doing a quick calculation in her mind, Lisa made a guess. "Valentine's Day?"

Nodding her head, "Yep" popped out of Liz's mouth. "Baby brothers can be so stubborn."

"You mean this isn't a temporary trait?"

"Afraid not. Don't get me wrong. He's poured his heart and soul into the tiniest of details. Yet ask him about practical things like bedding and towels, and he's clueless, and we won't even mention decorations. He's going to drive the rest of us crazy before this is over."

Lisa couldn't hold back the laughter, and before they knew it, both were commiserating over siblings. Their enjoyable conversation was interrupted by the master of the mansion.

Adam looked at the two of them disapprovingly, and the laughter stopped. "Liz, you and Kirk going to stay for lunch? I'm putting potatoes in the oven."

"You mean you haven't even fed Lisa lunch?"

Liz pushed herself up from the sofa and began to rail at her brother. "It's nearly two o'clock!"

Adam looked at Lisa and their eyes met. "She knows where the food is if she gets hungry."

"Adam MacIntyre!"

Lisa came to his defense. "He did tell me to help myself. I just lost track of time as I was exploring."

"See. She's not helpless," Adam added with a reluctant smile. "Either of you need anything before I get back to work? Food, drink, questions answered?"

"Oh, man. First you don't want a thing to do with this. Now—" she looked at Lisa "—you're dying to know just what secrets I'm telling. Tough, little brother. I'm handling this interview." She shooed him away as if he were a pesky ten-year-old. "You and Kirk go ahead with your chores. Remind my husband that we have dinner plans, but thanks for asking, Adam."

Lisa bit back a smile. Adam looked as if he'd just been sent to bed without supper. She listened to Liz talk, envisioning Adam happy and full of mischief, before she'd arrived.

"I don't know what's wrong with Adam, Lisa, but trust me, he isn't normally like this at all. I think the pressure is just starting to get to him. Why don't I give you the grand tour?"

"It's hard to imagine the magnitude of what he's taking on here." Lisa looked around, trying to imagine the room bustling with unfamiliar people.

"Adam is trying so hard to do this all on his own, but he just doesn't realize how much more there is to be done." After seeing the entire lodge, they returned to the great room and Lisa closed her notebook.

"I hope that helps." Liz handed her a business card. "If you need any help—with the interview, or my brother—just call."

Lisa nodded. "It's a beautiful building. Thank you for taking the time to show me around, Liz."

"I enjoyed it…and I'm thrilled that you're here to do this story for us. And despite Adam's sour mood, I think he's excited about this story, too." With that, Adam's sister left.

Despite Liz's claim, it was still difficult to picture Adam enjoying playing host. Or maybe he only found it impossible to be hospitable to *her*.

Whatever the reason, she was determined to change his mind.

Chapter Six

Adam went out of his way to avoid Lisa for the better part of the day. Allowing his sister to show Lisa around the guest house was probably the biggest mistake he could have made, and worse, they all knew it. Despite his efforts to ban Lisa from his mind, he'd been unable to keep his thoughts from drifting back to the blonde.

Glancing out the window, he spotted Lisa playing with Toby. She took him off the leash and threw a stick. Adam chuckled. Throws like a girl, all right. Poor Toby won't get much of a workout while she's around. Just then she took off running with the awkward puppy lumbering after her.

The steaks sizzled on the stovetop grill and bread warmed in the oven. He chopped a tomato and green pepper, tossed them into the lettuce, then topped it off with a handful of croutons.

The wind whistled as Lisa and Toby tromped inside. "Brrr. Looks like we're in for a storm." Her cheeks were pink. She tugged the fleece headband off and tucked it into her coat pocket. Spellbound, Adam watched her remove the scrunchie, comb her hair with her fingers, then magically twist the silken strands into one of those sloppy buns that were so popular.

Adam forced his attention back to dinner. "They're only predicting a couple of inches."

She smiled. "Just enough."

He waited for her to finish the sentence. "Just enough for what?"

She looked at him and shrugged. "To look pretty. Not enough to cause problems for the livestock or driving…. You know, just right."

He nodded, trying not to show his surprise at her thinking of the livestock. "Okay. Just enough." Don't get tangled up, ole boy. "Dinner will be ready in a few minutes. How do you like your steak?"

"Medium, please. What can I do?"

"I have it under control, but thanks."

When were both seated, he bowed his head to pray, noticing her reaction. Despite Lisa's hesitancy, Adam continued with his usual praise for the day and a blessing on the nourishment He'd provided.

"How'd the tour go?"

"This place is wonderful, Alex." She cut open her potato and added a tiny slice of butter, then sprinkled it with salt and pepper. He looked back at his own, drenched in both butter and sour cream.

He pushed the pottery dish toward her. "Sour cream?"

"No, but thanks." She smiled. "So you've been thinking about the article?"

Adam shrugged. "On the one hand, I don't mind free publicity, but on the other, it seems premature. I've planned to start slow this first year to give me the chance to see what works, what doesn't."

"And you're worried that the article will bring in too much business?"

"Isn't that the reason you're here?"

She took her time chewing. "The article won't be published until summer. As for reservations, you're the boss, so when you reach your limit, tell them you don't have any rooms available. What's the big deal?"

"You want me to lie?"

"It's not a lie. It's called knowing your limits. I've stayed at a lot of places that won't reserve all of their rooms. They hold one or two open for accidental overbookings, walk-ins or because they have less help or a busy schedule that week."

"How'd you find that out?"

Lisa smiled. "I'm a journalist. I ask a lot of questions. You never know where a story is lurking. Might even be a hidden article in Whispering Pines." She lifted her eyebrows.

Her eager smile almost melted his defenses. Almost. "I don't think so." He thought immediately how his sister's interference could turn his ranch into a romantic getaway if he wasn't careful.

"Oh, come on. Am I going to have to dig for the story—brothers, friends, old girlfriends…"

Though he knew she was teasing, just the mention of old girlfriends turned him cold. "I guess that depends on what kind of story you're after. You aren't the kind of journalist that would write anything to sell a story, are you?" He wanted to think he could trust Lisa, but then again, he'd trusted Amelia, and it had ended his career.

Raw hurt clouded her expression. "I wouldn't do that to you. Heavens, we're practically family."

Adam wanted to point out that her claim sounded a lot like a promise, but decided he'd best not press his luck. "*If* I agree, I want to approve the article before it goes to your editor."

"Okay, but I'm not going to miss a deadline if you're going to nitpick over minor details like word choice. You're going to have to trust me."

Trust. Adam thought a moment. One word could ruin everything. Ignoring the alarms going off in his head, he nodded.

"Great," she said, satisfaction sparkled in her eyes like stars on a moonless night. "I saw your mother leave. I hoped I could visit with her, too."

Adam wouldn't have minded that, either. Anything would have been preferable to facing temptation head-on all evening. "She volunteers every Saturday, then stays with Ricky and Alissa so Kevin and Emily can go out. We caravan back after church and Sunday dinner.''

''Sounds like a busy day.''

''We need to leave here at seven to make it to church on time.'' Adam took his last bite of steak.

Lisa had taken a bite at the same time and the silence loomed uncomfortably between them. ''I have a lot of work to do. I'll wait here while you go.''

''Your sisters are expecting you.''

She tucked her hair behind one ear. ''They'll get along just fine without me. You go ahead. I'll join you later,'' she repeated, this time more forcefully. She set her silverware down with a clang.

Adam didn't respond right away, hoping the silence would cool the discussion. ''Why didn't you say something then? I gave you the opening to decline.''

''They were in a hurry to leave.''

''You led them to believe you'd go to church.''

''There's one thing you may as well understand now, Adam. My sisters have families of their own…'' Lisa finished the last bite of steak, left the potato skins and carried her plate to the kitchen. ''I don't need to intrude on their lives.''

He could hear her loneliness. Adam followed her. ''You're family, Lisa. Of course they want you here.''

''Please don't get that 'poor Lisa' tone. They don't

need to take care of me. As far as that goes, they don't need me any more now than they ever did.''

"So you're saying…"

"I'm saying this really is none of your concern," she said as she pushed past him into the great room.

"Lisa, wait." He'd followed her. He knew that shock had to be written all over his face. "This morning was it? You're skipping the family dinner tomorrow just like during the holidays? Do you have any clue how disappointed your sisters were when you didn't come?"

"I was covering a Christmas story. Tell me that Emily won't ever have to work on a holiday, or that you're not going to have guests at Christmas. They don't have a corner on the market when it comes to disappointment." She wrapped a stray hair behind her ear. "But that's all history. Forgive and forget, seven thousand times over or some such nonsense, right?" The words tumbled carelessly from her lips. "Been there, tried that, didn't work, either."

Adam grabbed her arm as she started to leave. In an instant, he saw Lisa differently. She was no longer his sister-in-laws' self-centered little sister; she was a woman alone and in pain. "It's seventy times seven. What happened, Lisa?" He'd exposed a darker side to the drifter, and for the life of him, he didn't want to be the one to hear this. He shouldn't be asking in the first place. This was a discussion for her and her sisters. Everything within him warned him to let her go up those stairs and out of his life now.

"Let me go." She turned her head away.

Placing a finger on her chin, he turned her face toward his. Her eyes were wet and dark like the depths of the ocean she'd been watching the day before. It suddenly dawned on him that Lisa was nothing more than a tiny vessel lost at sea. He knew he should let go, but he couldn't loosen his grasp, as if he was somehow her anchor in the storm. "Come on, let's talk."

She tugged her arm and refused to look at him.

Adam didn't understand this desperate need to get involved. This morning he couldn't wait for her to leave. Tonight he was holding on, asking her to stay.

This is what Whispering Pines is for…a safe haven from life's storms. A place to get in touch with God. "Let's sit down." *Okay, God. Help me out here.* "We can talk, not talk, watch a movie, whatever you want." He released her arm slowly, half expecting her to run, half expecting to chase her down.

Lisa hesitated. She blinked once, and all traces of tears were gone. "I'll be fine."

She didn't sound fine, but he didn't dare say that. "I'm not. I'd like to understand."

"Understand what? You've already decided…"

"I never said such a thing. You're putting words in my mouth." Adam backed toward the sofa, not allowing his gaze to stray, just in case she bolted.

She lifted her chin. "Reading between the lines."

"Is that an occupational hazard?"

She burst out laughing, obviously as surprised as Adam at her response. Almost as quickly as the laughter had formed an invisible bond between them, he could see that ease replaced with fear.

He smiled, knowing he'd regret this later. "Come on, Lisa." For now he didn't want to think about later.

Lisa sat gingerly on the step to the foyer and unlaced her boots. "I'll be gone in a few days. You needn't worry about me and my sisters."

Adam eased his way closer and leaned an elbow on the antique conductor's ticket counter. "Emily and Katarina are *my* sisters now, too," he said, immediately wishing he could take the words back.

Lisa rolled her eyes. "And you want to be sure I don't hurt them."

"That's not what I meant exactly."

She stepped up next to the banister and gave him a cold hard stare. "What did you mean? Exactly."

Exactly, he couldn't say. Only that he cared for all of them more than he dared admit. He stared into Lisa's eyes, startled that he could almost imagine tasting her tears. Wished he could, exactly. "Exactly..." He'd get his face slapped if she knew.

She crossed her arms, pulling him back to the situation at hand.

"Exactly, I know how it is when things aren't right between sisters or brothers. I've seen how much

Emily and Kat missed you over the holidays. And now, I see that you're hurting, too.'' She didn't deny his claim. ''I may not be able to help, but I will listen.''

''Family is everything to you, Adam. I don't expect you to understand.''

''Try me.''

She started to say something, then shrugged and took a step up the stairs. ''It's nothing.''

''Lisa, I have two sisters, and trust me, our relationship is far from perfect. Liz probably told you more than I'd like you to know, but when we have a problem, we talk it out. This will stay between us.''

Toby lumbered into the room and looked at Lisa expectantly. She reached over to pet him. ''I love my sisters. I don't want you to get the wrong idea.''

''I know you do.'' Adam itched to move closer so he could offer her a friendly hug, but held his ground.

Lisa moved to the hearth and simply petted the dog, ignoring Adam completely.

Adam waited in painful silence. Toby came to him and let out a deep yip, his way of asking to go out. When Adam returned, Lisa had moved to the sofa.

''This morning you accused me of always running,'' she said.

He wasn't sure what to answer. He couldn't take it back. ''It's the truth, isn't it? You were barely here long enough for each of your sister's weddings.''

Lisa lifted her chin. ''Did they say that?''

''No, they didn't, but I'm not blind. You didn't

come home for the past two Christmases, or Thanksgiving or Easter—or at all,'' Adam said.

She let out an audible protest. ''That's not true. I spent a week with Mom and my sisters at the cabin before Kevin and Emily decided to get married. I was here right before Christmas for Kat and Alex's wedding. This year, I worked. Besides, this isn't home,'' she argued.

''I think of home as where my family is, you know, like we come 'home' from college, whether it be to Grandpa's, or Mom's, or Susan's... Your mom even came.''

''Why wouldn't she? Now that both Emily and Kat are here...'' She lowered her head slightly.

Adam could see her eyes mist over and wished he'd kept his mouth shut. ''My mom says it's easier for her to travel than it is with kids. I'm sure Naomi would have stayed home if you'd asked.''

Lisa shook her head. ''It doesn't matter. Mom's house isn't home, either.'' She looked at him, startled, as if she'd revealed some deep dark secret.

''It may not be the same house, but...''

''My sophomore year of college, Mom left a note on the door, telling me to meet her at some new address. I tried my key in our house, but it didn't work.'' Lisa tugged the ponytail holder from her hair and let it fall loose around her face. ''Mom finally had a good job and celebrated by getting rid of everything—the house and most everything inside.''

''Wow.'' The single word escaped, followed by a

small whistle. The silence between them multiplied, made more miserable by the fact that he couldn't think of any comforting words to say.

She pulled her knees close to her chest and rested her chin upon her hands. "I never begrudged Mom a nice place or the chance to start over. She deserved it after what my father put her through."

"He abandoned all of you, Lisa."

She let out a soft sigh. "I was two when he left. Emily and Kat were the ones who had to take care of their pesky little sister. They were responsible for fixing meals and putting me to bed while Mom worked. When they went to college, Mom was only working one job and taking night classes. So you see, home wasn't all warm and filled with love and comfort. Without my sisters, it was a roof over my head. I don't ever plan to burden them again."

"Lisa..." Adam reached out to comfort her, but Toby's bark caught Lisa's attention.

"May I let him in? It must be terribly cold out there." She obviously welcomed the interruption.

"Sure." Adam didn't bother to tell her that Alex had built the dog a well-insulated doghouse. Lisa needed a distraction from the conversation and so did he. He wanted to assure her that she could always count on family, but now wasn't the time. He wasn't technically her relative, and he knew that getting too involved was a bad idea. He'd been telling himself that ever since Katarina and Alex's wedding, when he'd seen her dancing in front of that mirror.

She was hurting, and he knew her only true healing could come from the one source she seemed to be turning her back on—God.

Lisa let the overzealous puppy inside. She knelt down, inviting the dog give her a sloppy wet kiss. "Good dog. Let's show your dad how well we're doing." She replaced his rope with the short training leash. "Toby, heel." Lisa led him into the living room.

"Toby and I found your training manual this afternoon while you were tending the cattle."

He lifted his eyebrows. "Really?" They were about as mismatched as any dog and owner could be. She was graceful as a deer, and Toby as overbearing as a bull in a china closet.

"We did. He does very well." She held her hand in front of the dog. "Sit, Toby." Her commanding voice sounded too sweet and feminine for a dog to take seriously. Toby looked at Adam with a gaze that begged for sympathy. Adam forced a straight face.

"Toby, sit," Lisa repeated more sternly. Toby hesitated, then dropped his rump onto the hardwood floor. "Good dog," she crooned.

Her admiration distracted the dog, and his tail end was wagging even before his rump left the floor. "Toby, sit." Lisa stood straight. "Sit, Toby!" It was too late. Toby lunged at Adam, dragging Lisa along.

Adam could see what was coming, but for the life of him, he couldn't stop it. He just hoped there would be no injuries and that he'd be able to keep a straight face.

Lisa finally let go of the leash just as the dog launched onto the couch and right over the back.

"Toby!" Adam reached out to catch the dog and found his arms around Lisa. "This beats Toby anyday."

Facing him, she squirmed, trying to get up.

"Relax a minute," Adam whispered, resting his fingers on her shoulder. "Look at Toby. He's looking at us like he had this all planned."

She turned toward the dog. "The rascal."

"You okay?" He extended his arm, folding his hand around her shoulder.

"I'm fine. I could use some help up."

He simply stared at her. The color of her eyes. The way her silky hair framed her face. "You don't have to run, Lisa."

Her gaze met his, and the distance between them disappeared. She jumped when he touched her hair.

Still unable to get her balance, Lisa pushed herself off the sofa. "Don't complicate things, Adam."

"What?"

She picked herself up, straightened her sweater and brushed the hair from her flushed face.

"I'm sorry, Lisa." He jumped off the couch and took a step toward her.

She backed away. "It's my fault. I shouldn't have shared those things with you. After all, I'm here on business. I think we'd both be wise to remember that."

He felt as if someone had opened the door and let the cold wind shock him back to reality. She was right. Asking a drifter to stay was like asking the wind not to blow. "What about tomorrow?"

"I'll go to Kat's for dinner, but that's all."

"Springville is forty miles away, so if you want to go to dinner, we go to church, too."

"Forty miles?"

Adam nodded. "I expect you to be ready by seven."

"And if I'm not?"

"I'll come and get you." He walked to the back of the house before she could argue. She wanted to stick to business? Fine. He'd show her business.

Chapter Seven

Adam was surprised to see Lisa waiting at the kitchen table when he came out of his private quarters the next morning. "Changed your mind, huh?"

"No, but I do want to see my sisters. I put a plate in the oven for you." She looked at her watch and raised her eyebrows. "By my guess, you have seven minutes before we need to leave."

"I overslept," he grumbled. "I couldn't leave chores for later."

"And you were worried about me," she teased, a secretive smile softening the mood. "What would you like to drink?"

"I can get it. You didn't need to fix me any breakfast, but thanks." Adam pulled the plate from the oven and poured himself a tall glass of orange juice.

"Well, I'll admit, I'm way out of practice in the

kitchen, but I figured I couldn't do much to mess up sausage and scrambled eggs.''

''They look great.'' Adam took a fork and nearly shoveled the food into his mouth. How could she be so cheery after acting as if he'd done something so terribly wrong just the night before? He finished with two minutes to spare. ''Let's go.''

She picked up a notebook and grabbed the shoulder strap of her camera bag.

''Here, let me get that for you.'' Adam reached for the bag. ''My back hurts just watching you lift it.''

Lisa smiled as she set the strap onto her shoulder. ''This is nothing compared to those I carried in school. Mine isn't even full yet. I only have one extra camera body and three lenses.''

''Only?''

''Once I can afford it, I'll have three or four bodies and at least five lenses, depending on the type of photography I'm doing.''

''May as well order a caddy to lug it all around for you while you're at it.''

''Thanks anyway, but I prefer to work solo,'' she said.

Wet snow fell fast and furious, melting as soon as it hit the ground. They'd driven nearly thirty minutes on dirt roads when Adam began having trouble steering. He pulled the truck to a stop and opened his door and leaned out to look. ''We have a flat tire.''

He set the emergency brake and shut off the engine, then yanked the tie from around his neck.

Lisa held up the strip of fabric and smiled. "Somehow I wouldn't have pictured you as a Tweety kind of guy. Yosemite Sam, maybe, Deputy Dawg, definitely a possibility...but Tweety? No. Now maybe Sylvester fits..."

He shot her an unappreciative glance and took the keys from the ignition. "Ricky gave it to me for Christmas. He picked it out himself."

She dropped the tie, trying to subdue a smile. "I see. It's adorable. Can I do anything to help?"

"Call one of your sisters and tell them not to plan on us sitting with them in church. My cell phone is in the glove box." He grabbed a pair of leather gloves from under the seat and closed the door, shutting out the icy wind and snowflakes, as well as his bad mood. The weather turned worse by the minute.

Lisa opened the glove box to search for his phone. She found it neat and organized, paperwork in a plastic file and a small clear box filled with little screws and assorted pieces. Who would have thought Adam to be one of those people who had a place for everything and actually kept everything in its place?

She found the phone and gave Katarina a quick overview of the morning's mishaps while Adam paced from the front of the truck to the back, pulling things from the metal box behind the cab. A minute later, she saw him set a handful of bolts on the hood of the truck, then felt the vehicle tilt to one side.

From Adam's efficiency and the fancy tools he had on hand, she guessed changing flat tires to be a regular occurrence for the rugged cowboy.

She regretted that there was nothing she could do to help, especially when Adam crawled back into the truck with mud-caked boots and splattered clothes.

She'd never seen Adam such a mess, even in his work clothes. He pulled the gloves off, then reached behind the seat and pulled out a rag to wipe the dirt from his dress pants.

Lisa opened her mouth to suggest they turn around and head back to Whispering Pines, but before she could, he started the truck and continued down the road. She would love nothing more than to go back to the ranch and spend the day there. She also knew better than to say so after their discussion the previous night. If she had to sit in the truck through the service in order to keep the peace between them, so be it. She needed this story. A year without a permanent job was growing old, not to mention not having a place to call home. Every time she thought she had a job and was ready to sign a lease, something went wrong.

She had it so much better than most of the homeless people she'd met. By her own opinion, she wasn't really homeless at all. True, she didn't have a permanent residence, but she'd never spent one night without a roof over her head. Her contacts in the publishing world had kept her busy enough to replace her equipment and set aside adequate travel funds. By most standards, she'd be considered an incredibly successful freelancer. Only problem was, she wanted the security of a full-time job, a monthly paycheck and a place to unpack her bags, permanently.

Adam asked Lisa about her travels, most likely out of boredom or a sense of obligation. Either way, it helped fill the awkward silence between them. The only other noise was the murmur of the radio, which took precedence over conversation when the weather alert came on, upgrading the forecast to a winter storm warning.

Adam looked at his watch as he pulled into the church parking lot. "The service is nearly half over but Mike probably hasn't started his sermon yet. You sure you don't want to come?"

"I'll wait out here."

"If you're upset about last night, I'm sorry." Adam fumbled with the silken strip of fabric until he had it tied into knots. "Don't worry. It won't happen again."

Just hearing the words from his mouth made her heart do a little dance. Had he truly been ready to kiss her? Lisa felt a huge sigh of relief escape. She'd scolded herself all night for overreacting. "Well, I'm happy to know I wasn't imagining things."

Adam tipped the rearview mirror down so he could see what he was doing. "At least one of us is happy." He slipped the knot up to his throat and straightened the two strips of fabric.

"So just because I didn't let you kiss me, we're going to be at each other's throats again?"

"And just because I was crazy enough to care about you for a few minutes, you think you can get what you want by flirting?"

"Flirting? With you?" She straightened her back and turned toward him. "I was just trying to keep the peace, joke around a bit..."

"Well, don't. Tomorrow you ask your questions, take your pictures and get on the road." He opened the door. "I'm going to church, then Bible fellowship. See you later."

Adam stopped in the men's rest room on his way into the church hoping to clean up. Looking in the mirror, he realized it was no use. Other than chipping the mud from his face, there was little he could do. His clothes were a disaster. If it hadn't been for Lisa's presence, he would have turned around after the flat tire. He hadn't been about to let her win this argument. Lot of good his stubbornness did him. It was either attend services as he was, or go out to the truck with Lisa and wait for church to end.

Why is it that the only woman I've been remotely interested in in three years is the one woman who wants nothing to do with You, me or my ranch, Lord?

There was no decision to be made. He eased the door to the sanctuary open and slipped through as quietly as he could.

"Morning, Adam," Pastor Mike said from the pulpit. "Looks like the truck won." A soft ripple of laughter spread through the congregation. "Glad you're here safe."

So much for sneaking in without being noticed. He found a seat and spotted Alex and Katarina. She turned awkwardly in her seat and mouthed, "Where's Lisa?"

He pretended to put his hands on the steering wheel and drive, then shrugged. Even from halfway across the room he could see her disappointment.

"This morning's scripture is from Matthew 18, verses twelve to fourteen, the parable of the lost sheep." Mike directed the congregation to the pages in the pew Bibles, then recited the verses.

"Is there a lost sheep in your life? Your family? Your workplace?" Pastor Mike paused, and a hush came over the room. "What about in our church? Could there be a lost sheep sitting in the pew next to you?"

The sermon was hard-hitting, making Adam all too aware of his own failings. Especially when the lost sheep was someone he cared for. Particularly when caring guaranteed being hurt.

Adam's mind raced with thoughts of what he should do. Things he should say. He felt dots of perspiration bead on his forehead. He'd never been comfortable pushing his beliefs on others. He'd seen what preaching at someone had done to his cousin Chance—turned him as far away from a relationship with God as anyone could go. Instead, Adam tried to show his faith through his own actions. Somehow that didn't seem like enough.

When Mike closed his sermon in prayer, Adam added his own personal request for intervention. Divine or otherwise—just so God didn't ask Adam to try to get through to Lisa. When the service was over, he stepped to the side, allowing the others to go on by.

Katarina made a beeline for him, leaving Alex far behind. "Adam, where's Lisa?"

"I tried to convince her to come in, but she refused. More than once." He thought of the night before, afraid that sharing Lisa's comments with her sister could create more tension. "She seemed... uncomfortable..."

"I know. Something's happened and she won't share it with anyone. Ever since the wedding she's seemed...well...lost." Katarina shrugged. "Did you notice, the title of his sermon was supposed to be on forgiveness? I can't believe the timing. Lisa surprises us by dropping in and Mike's lesson is on lost sheep."

He was glad Lisa's sister recognized the situation. "Quite a coincidence, huh?"

"Coincidence, my foot. God brought her here for a reason. So how's He supposed to work if she won't even come to church?"

He shrugged. "She didn't say specifically why. She just refused to come in. And I thought you and Emily could be stubborn."

"We're not stubborn...." Katarina grinned. "A little on the determined side maybe."

"Whatever you say...I still call it stubborn, especially when it comes to Lisa."

Alex made his way through the crowd and rubbed his wife's shoulders. Katarina patted her round belly. "Alex, would you mind if we go home? I didn't sleep well last night, and I'd like to spend more time with Lisa. She's sitting in the truck."

Alex chuckled. "No problem. I'll go tell Mom and Kevin to come to the house whenever they're ready."

"We'll be right over." Adam didn't linger, anxious to get back home. With any luck at all, he'd be able to convince his houseguest that she'd be more comfortable spending the remainder of her time in Colorado with one of her sisters.

He stepped outside, snow and icy wind slapping him in the face. Lisa had to be freezing. How could he have left her sitting in a cold vehicle in the middle of a blizzard? Dodging incoming churchgoers bundled in winter coats and boots, he hurried through the parking lot.

Adam wasn't at all happy with the message he kept hearing. God couldn't be serious. Adam didn't need someone in his life, and Lisa didn't want to settle down. "She may be your lost sheep, Lord, but I'm not going to be the shepherd. This is one stray that has no intention of staying with her flock."

The wind chilled Adam's neck and snow pelted

his skin. He glanced at the cars as he walked past. Windshields were iced over. A good inch of snow had fallen since he'd gone into the church less than an hour ago.

When he arrived at the pickup, he wiped the snow from the windshield with his leather glove. She had to be freezing cold and madder than—

He swiped his hand over the passenger's side window....

She was gone.

He took off his glove, pulled his keys from his pocket and searched the interior of the truck for an explanation. There was none. He slammed the door and looked around.

Church traffic had packed down the snow around his truck, leaving no hope of following her footprints. He ran back into the building and looked around, hoping that she'd gone inside, if for no better reason than to stay warm. After checking the reception area, he returned to the foyer.

He glanced up at the chandelier, remembering the snowy December night when Katarina's bridal bouquet had caught in that very lamp. The memory was quickly replaced with the one of him and Lisa vowing no one would ever find out that each of them had caught a section of those flowers. Unfortunately, he hadn't been able to get her out of his mind since.

Pushing the memory away, he ran up the stairs and peeked into each classroom, hoping that by some miracle, he'd find her.

After searching for half an hour, Adam finally called his brother's house. "Hey, Alex. Did Lisa catch up with you and Katarina on your way out of church?"

"No. I thought she was waiting in your truck."

"I thought so, too, but she's…" He felt a pang of guilt, remembering the way he'd spoken to her before he abandoned her. "Well, she's not there."

His brother's voice lowered to a near whisper. "Where is she?"

"If I knew, would I be calling you?" Adam snapped. "Never mind, I'll find her." He dropped the phone onto the base, thanked the church secretary and headed back outside.

"It is not the will of the Father that any of His lost sheep shall perish." Pastor Mike's sermon packed a powerful message that Adam wasn't all that happy about at the moment. Adam had to find his lost sheep. Lisa.

Chapter Eight

Adam looked down the street. Most of the stores were closed. He glanced the other direction toward a school and a beauty shop, both of which would be closed on a Sunday. He headed toward the business district, zipped his coat and unfolded the collar.

Half an hour later he found her sitting in a coffee shop several blocks away, reading the newspaper.

"Ahem." Adam leaned one hand on the extra chair.

She lifted her gaze to his gloved hand and quickly followed his arm up to his face. Her eyes widened. "Adam!" Lisa looked at her watch. "I didn't think class would be out so early." She guzzled the remainder of her latte.

"It isn't. I—Katarina..." he stammered. "Because of the weather we decided to skip class today.

This storm is getting worse. I need to head back to the ranch.''

She folded the paper and jumped from her chair. "I'm sorry. I didn't dream you'd be done so soon." Lisa yanked her coat from the back of the bentwood chair and Adam found himself holding it for her while she put it on. "I planned to meet you back at the truck before eleven."

Despite his anger, he remained calm. "I was afraid I'd said something to send you running."

She turned toward him and her eyes brightened with merriment. "It takes a lot more than a little growling to chase me away. Haven't you figured that out yet?" She zipped her coat and pulled the hood over her head.

"I guess you've made that clear. Haven't you?" Adam wasn't sure whether to be angry at her or himself. At Lisa for not giving up on the story, or himself for being cowardly enough to wish she would.

A few minutes later, Adam pulled into Katarina and Alex's driveway feeling more unsure of himself than he had in years. He wondered if it would be terribly rude to drop her off and head home. Right now he didn't even care if it was. He just wanted to wake up three days earlier, before Lisa walked back into his life and rekindled dreams he thought he'd put to rest permanently.

While Katarina eagerly escorted Lisa inside, Adam slipped his boots off on the front porch to keep from getting their brand-new house muddy. Kevin met

Adam at the door and handed him a stack of clothes. "Thought you might need these," Kevin said, examining Adam's pants. "Where in the world did you and that tire have the run-in anyway?"

Adam tucked the bundle under his arm. "South of Elk Creek Draw. Thanks for bringing these. I'll be right back." He tiptoed through the kitchen to the mudroom and closed the door, shutting out the joyous sounds of the family reunion.

Walking up to the house, Adam wished he and Lisa had met in another time, another place. He wished family connections weren't so strong. Even showing a casual interest could lead to a lifetime of awkward family gatherings. In that regard, he had probably already blown it last night when he'd almost kissed her.

When he'd finished dressing, Adam considered asking Alex for a different pair of jeans. Surely his wouldn't be so snug, even if Adam did have to roll the legs like a kid wearing hand-me-downs.

Adam moved around a bit, then pulled the flannel shirt on and buttoned it, leaving it untucked. Maybe no one would notice. He looked around the adjoining laundry room, picked up a spray bottle then misted the jeans with water and knelt down to stretch them. After rolling his muddy slacks into a bundle, Adam wrapped them inside the less-soiled shirt. He opened the door to the kitchen. "Katarina, do you have a bag for these muddy pants and shirt?"

Lisa was the only one in the room.

She gave him the once-over and bit her lower lip, as if to hide her smile.

"Don't you dare say a word," he growled.

"I was just thinking I never have my camera when I need it," she said in a deliberate whisper. Lisa pulled open one cupboard, then another. Then, her voice louder, she said, "I'm sure Kat has an extra grocery sack around here someplace." Finally she found the right cupboard and handed him one, a smile blatantly teasing her lips.

"Not a word." He dropped the clothes inside, then immediately distanced himself, hoping to shake this feeling. Lisa wasn't his type. Once she had what she wanted, she'd be gone.

Kevin stomped the snow from his loafers and handed Katarina the salad. "I think we'd better cut the afternoon short so Adam and Lisa can get back to the ranch. This storm isn't letting up."

Adam went to the sliding door and looked to the west. "That may not be such a bad idea. Why don't I let Lisa stay and I'll…"

Emily stood immediately and stopped him. "Nonsense. We'll have dinner on in a jiffy. Why don't you and Kevin keep the kids occupied?" Alex finished setting the table and sliced the ham.

In a matter of minutes, dinner was served, and everyone rushed to the table. By the time Adam made his way to the table, there were two seats left. One next to Lisa, or one across from her. *You couldn't cut me some slack here, could you, God?*

His mother moved past him with the last serving dish and chose the chair across from Lisa, eliminating his options. With lead feet, Adam walked around the table and sat down.

"Let's pray," Alex said. Everyone took hold of the hand of the person seated next to him and set it on the table. Adam could see Lisa's discomfort as the awkwardness stretched between them.

"C'mon, Aunt Lisa. We hafta hold hands." Her nephew raised his hand to her, and she forced a smile.

"Sorry," she muttered, taking Ricky's hand in hers.

Adam reached out, taking hold of her other hand, and Alex proceeded with a lengthy blessing for the food, the much-needed moisture, Lisa's safe journey and anything else one could imagine. Finding it difficult to concentrate on the prayer instead of the woman next to him, Adam silently added his own request for God to heal Lisa's pain.

He wasn't sure how he survived the meal, but he couldn't deny he was more than relieved when it was over.

After they'd cleared the dishes, Millie insisted Adam and Lisa get going. His mother explained that she'd be staying the week to help Katarina finish a large shipment of dolls and help Emily get ready for Alissa's first birthday. Millie looked at Adam as if daring him to argue.

"If you'd rather stay here..." Adam said.

"Oh, no, I couldn't..." Lisa rambled on with a full explanation and ended it with a quick goodbye.

By the time they'd reached the highway, Lisa started asking questions as if her entire intention had been to corner him. "What made you open the ranch to the public?"

Adam hedged, instinct telling him to give her as little information as possible. Maybe, just maybe, there was still a chance she would give up. "I was already hosting friends and their friends who wanted a quiet place to get away. They seemed to like having someplace close to home, but away from the city. It seemed natural to make the business official."

She asked another question, and he gave her a clipped response.

"What activities do you plan to offer? Or do you plan to let guests find their own entertainment?"

"Horseback rides, chuck-wagon dinners, hay rides, fishing. If we have enough snow, sleigh rides, cross-country skiing, snowmobiling, snowshoeing... The possibilities are endless." From the corner of his eye he could see her smile. "What's so funny?"

She let out a soft husky laugh. "Nothing. Am I making you nervous?"

"What makes you think that?"

"You're so tense," she said softly.

Guilt hit him like a hoof in his gut. All the woman wanted was a story and he was treating her like she was out to take him for all he was worth. Adam didn't need this reminder of Amelia, or the investigation. "The roads are terrible."

"Would you rather we continue this later?"

Did he detect a flirtatious challenge in her voice? He resented her taking advantage of the slow drive home to bombard him with questions, and doubly resented that she could tell the interview was getting to him. He shoved the reminders of his past to the back of his mind. "No, go ahead."

She hesitated. "How do you feel about opening your home to strangers? Won't you miss your privacy?"

He had to hand it to the woman. Her questions teetered on the edge of personal, but the way she asked them, they technically focused on business. He'd deliberately ignored those personal issues. He had no choice. The ranch needed an income besides cattle to cover expenses. Ranching just wasn't enough nowadays. This was a business move he'd had to make, despite his personal hesitancy.

"Adam?" She looked at him with wide blue eyes.

Keep your mind on business, old boy. If he could just find a way to tighten the reins on his attraction, they could both get on with their lives. Knowing the problem had to be half the battle, he reasoned. If Lisa wasn't interested, why was he? "What does my privacy have to do with your article? Maybe it's time I ask your plans for this story."

She grimaced. "Well..."

"'Well' isn't a good bargaining chip right now, Lisa."

She snapped her notebook closed. "Why don't we finish this later?"

"Why don't you answer *my* questions this time? I deserve to know. After all, this is about my ranch."

Lisa stalled. "I want you to understand, this isn't my idea. I can show you her e-mail to prove it."

"'Her'?" Adam took a quick glance at Lisa. "Give it to me straight. What does 'she' want?"

"My editor wants to focus on the romantic getaway, and…you. About why a single cowboy—"

"Hold it right there." Adam slowed to a stop at the traffic light, holding his temper in check. Why was it that the Lord kept throwing him into situations where business and romance repeatedly became twisted as tight as jute rope? Adam thought he'd finally found a way to avoid getting his professional life all tangled up with his personal life and along came Lisa Berthoff. "Romance is out, and while you're at it, you can leave me out of it, too."

"But…"

He flashed her a firm but gentle warning. "Those are my terms. Take them, or leave them."

Lisa's gaze didn't stray. "I'll make it work."

Lisa spent the remainder of the afternoon trying to figure out just how to satisfy both Adam and her editor. She knew Adam wouldn't like any article that put too much emphasis on him, yet her editor wanted a story about the romance of the ranch setting and the single cowboy owner. What a mess.

As soon as they'd arrived, Adam had changed clothes, started a load of laundry, then disappeared.

She found a cozy seat in the corner of the great room and tried to work. She scribbled a few notes, then erased them and gazed out the window. Every now and then, she caught a glimpse of Adam. Whether tossing bales of hay from the back of his truck or giving Toby commands, his every movement exuded masculinity.

He was a man at peace with himself. Everything seemed to go the way he wanted. Did Adam have any clue of the treasure he had here in his retreat from the world? A whiff of burning pine and one look around the spacious lodge, and she realized she was in trouble.

Lisa shook off the sensation of envy that tended to creep into her consciousness whenever she slowed down for too long. She couldn't cave in now. She had to stay strong. Had to prove to her mother and sisters and her louse of a father that she had what it took to succeed. She wouldn't ever let herself depend on anyone else for support.

Lisa paced, trying to deny the fact that Adam held her future in his hands. The article had the potential to go to several markets, not just for romantic getaways. The key to success in freelancing was to cover every angle in one interview. A little tweak, and the piece was salable to at least a dozen markets, a fact she didn't dare share with Adam right now.

Just thinking of him, her heartbeat quickened. She recalled his arms around her, and her face warmed. Much as she tried to tell her emotions that he had only been doing what anyone would have if his dog was mauling someone, it wasn't working. There was something dangerously different about Adam.

Despite girlish dreams, Lisa knew better than to think there was a man on the face of the earth who wouldn't leave her brokenhearted. Dale had. And even her own father had turned his back on her. She pulled her knees close to her body and much as she resisted, the tears seeped through.

The phone at the check-in counter rang, and Lisa hesitated. When it rang the fifth time, Lisa finally answered. "Whispering Pines Guest Ranch."

"Millie?" The feminine voice sounded concerned.

"No, she's not available. May I take a message?" Lisa wiped the tears onto her sleeve and dug through the train conductor's stand for paper and pencil.

"Well, then, who is this? Adam's sister?" The voice turned from irritated to sweet, as if the caller was suddenly trying to make a good impression.

Lisa tried to hold on to her patience while her irritation continued to grow. Adam hadn't mentioned a girlfriend. "No. How may I direct your call?"

"Oh," the caller said snippily. "I must have missed your name."

Now Lisa was feeling an uncommon twinge of

orneriness. The woman was jealous. Lisa wanted to laugh. "No, you didn't. May I tell Adam who called? He's busy at the moment."

The woman hesitated. "This is Tara. Have him call me back as soon as possible. Adam has the number," she purred. "I'm calling to confirm our lunch date for tomorrow."

Lisa's hand paused after "lunch date." "I'll give him the message." Lisa hung up, feeling her smile fade as confusion set in. Despite trying not to care about the stubborn cowboy, she did. And it just figured that there was already another woman in his life. She should have known better than to trust him.

She strolled across the room to the box of tissues and grabbed a handful as a flood of memories raced her tears for release. She recalled the day she and Dale had moved across the country together, and the day two months later that she'd come home from Katarina's wedding to find all of her possessions gone along with the man she'd thought loved her. She'd cried for hours that night in the empty apartment, kicking herself for turning down a promising job for a man she barely knew.

Apparently, even God had lost His patience with her and was showing His disapproval through the trials she'd experienced this past year. Why should He be any different than any other man in her life had been?

Drying her tears, Lisa realized it was nearly dark

and Adam hadn't returned. She found a muffin in the refrigerator and warmed it in the microwave.

Adam's accusations lingered in her thoughts as she nibbled on a juicy blueberry and sipped a glass of milk. "Yeah, Adam, I run, and I'll keep on running. It's the only protection I have."

She went to work on her laptop, frustrated that Adam wouldn't cooperate. Apparently the man didn't appreciate the value of free national exposure, she thought bitterly. Letting her anger replace her logic, she pounded out an article sure to please her editor. Now all she needed to complete the assignment were a few pictures and she could be on the road again.

The snow had stopped, yet the wind whistled in the stovepipe. Out the picture window she could see the lights from town reflecting off the ominous, hovering clouds. Where could Adam be?

Adam blamed his edginess on the storm, claiming he was anxious to check to be sure everything was okay. Was that really why he seemed so angry? Or was it the story? Or her? All afternoon she had been walking a fine line between making amends and what Adam might misconstrue as flirting.

The clock chimed. Moonlight glistened over the fresh layer of snow. She tugged on her boots and coat, grabbed her camera and headed outside. This was a shot she couldn't miss.

Chapter Nine

Adam was relieved to see an end to the snow. It had been a long day of bitterly cold winds. Only good part about it was the winds had blown the storm away. The last thing he needed this week was a foot of snow. He slammed the iron rod against the solid barrier, determined to chip a hole in the ice. The pond had frozen over little more than a week ago, and keeping enough of it open for watering the stock had become a full-time job.

Adam resigned himself to the fact that Lisa would be here for a few more days. Her mission wouldn't be complete until she had her article.

He'd spent most of the afternoon trying to figure out just exactly what God seemed to think Adam could do for Lisa. And while he was at it, he wished God would confirm His plans for the ranch, too. The only thing Adam was absolutely sure of was that he belonged at Whispering Pines. The scandalous end to his investment career had stripped him of trust, his self-confidence and nearly his faith. Thanks to his grandfather's legacy, Adam had found a resting place and his inner peace restored.

Now that the time had come to open the lodge, Adam was having second thoughts that his investment would pay off. He lifted his head and scanned the property.

Toby took off across the pond and Adam looked up to make sure the dog made it okay. The ice was barely thick enough to support the hundred-pound puppy.

The shock of discovery hit him full force when he saw Lisa standing almost at the middle of the pond taking a picture. "Lisa, go back!"

He dropped the rod and pointed toward the lodge. "Go on! What are you doing out here?" He waved his hands. "Get out of here! Go back!"

Lisa let the camera drop against her body and watched as Toby lumbered to greet her.

"Hurry up!" Adam picked up his pace rounding the perimeter of the pond. "That ice isn't thick enough to support both you and Toby at once!"

Realization must have finally hit her as Lisa spun around and followed her own footprints. Toby caught up with her and Adam heard the ice crack.

She took two more steps with Toby at her heels before it gave.

Adam hit the split-rail fence at a full run and jumped it like a gymnast over the pommel horse.

Lisa stumbled as the ice disappeared beneath her feet, then fell to her hands and knees at the edge of the shore. She was safe.

Thank you, God.

Just then there was another splash. Toby stepped too close to the hole Lisa's foot had made and disappeared.

"Toby," she wailed.

"No! Lisa, don't."

Lisa turned, then slipped. Ignoring the frigid water, she lunged forward and grabbed for the dog. Seconds later she threw herself backward, tugging Toby by his collar from the deeper water to safety.

Adam helped haul Toby to shore, then pulled the sopping wet woman to her feet. Without pause, he lifted her into his arms and headed back to the lodge before she caught her death of cold. "What in the world were you doing out here?" he demanded, plowing as fast as he could through the freshly fallen snow.

"I was taking pictures. Don't tell me you missed the moon."

He looked around. "The what?" The woman had come close to drowning and she was talking about the moon?

"You've been out here all evening and missed that beautiful moon? Tell me you're joking." She squirmed and he tightened his grip.

Toby shook the water from his fur and let out a friendly bark, then jumped up.

"Stay down, Toby," Adam commanded.

"Don't yell at him. It's not his fault."

The woman was going to drive him insane if she didn't kill them all first. "I'll yell at both of you. That was a stupid thing to do."

"I had no idea there was a pond there," she argued. "It looked like a flat meadow. After all, you were standing there."

Adam stopped and looked into her misty eyes, kicking himself for the way he was treating her.

She struggled against him. "I'm perfectly capable of making it back on my own, Adam MacIntyre."

Even in the midst of a crisis she remained calm, determined and focused on her goal. He admired that. With the force of being bucked off a bronc, he realized just how much he admired her. How much he cared about her. How much it had scared him to see her walking across that thin ice.

He let Lisa's legs slide from his hold, keeping one arm around her waist. He brushed the wet hair from her face and covered her mouth with his, feeling warmth return to her quivering lips. His heart beat wildly against his chest.

Lisa's safe. Thank you, Father.

For what seemed like forever, they stood, tangled in each other's embrace, as if sharing an emotional kiss could keep her warm against the cold Colorado air. He didn't want to let her go, and kissed her again, slow and tenderly. Adam backed away and looked into her wide eyes. What am I doing? "I'm sorry, Lisa," he whispered. "You scared the daylights out of me."

She pulled away, turned and ran.

Chapter Ten

Adam let her run. She wouldn't go far. Not this time anyway.

He swept the back of his wet glove across his mouth, as if that could erase what had happened. He slowly followed Lisa and Toby's tracks to the lodge. What in the world had possessed him, kissing her like that? He knew better. Lisa Berthoff was off-limits.

The picture of Lisa and Toby falling through the ice played again and again in his mind like a recurring nightmare.

She's okay. Let it go.

Adam glanced over his shoulder, toward the pond.

If he'd been thinking beyond the renovation of the lodge all of this could have been prevented. He hadn't thought of the dangers ahead of time. A sign. A fence. Any number of barriers could have prevented the accident. This time he was lucky. What if he hadn't been there?

Lisa had looked so vulnerable, yet she had remained strong and courageous, thinking of his dog's safety above her own. She obviously didn't know the Newfoundland breed was once used primarily for water rescue on the high seas.

Could she ever forgive his negligence? His yelling? His bullheadedness? Any apology he could offer now would sound lame.

And that kiss. It shook him, no doubt about it. No matter how much the accident affected him, kissing her did nothing but complicate an already rotten situation. It had nothing to do with apologizing and everything with wanting her. Yet Lisa wasn't the type to stick around, and he wasn't the type to let her go. Relationships were difficult enough when both people were in the same town. He couldn't imagine trying to keep one going with one person wandering the country.

She's a drifter. Maybe if he said it often enough, he'd convince himself that he was only kidding himself to imagine otherwise. Lisa didn't have roots, and furthermore, didn't want them. Her running proved it. No matter how badly he wanted to taste her sweet lips again, it wouldn't happen. He'd make certain of that. He wouldn't let his weakness keep her away from upcoming family holidays. He had to straighten things out between them, before it was too late.

He stepped in the door, took the leather gloves

from his hands and tossed them onto the kitchen counter. Toby's tail thumped a greeting, and Adam pushed his own problems aside. He tugged off his boots and hung his coat on the wooden peg in the mudroom, then returned with some old towels. Slowly and gently he rubbed the dog's fur, rewarded by the dog's wet tongue on his rough cheek.

"Yeah, yeah, I love you, too, you rascal." He patted the dog and led him across the kitchen to a spot near the stove. "Stay, Toby, stay." He slowly backed away, pleased when the dog lowered his head onto his front paws and looked at Adam as if saying, "You couldn't drag me away."

Adam went upstairs to apologize to Lisa. When he heard the water running, he realized she must still be in the shower trying to warm up. Retreating, he hoped she'd still be speaking to him when she came out.

It had been a long day. Under normal circumstances, he'd follow his shower with a soak in the hot tub on the back porch. Not tonight. There was no way he could relax after all that had happened.

Before he cleaned up, Adam started a pot of vegetable beef soup. After browning the hamburger and onions, he added a can of tomato juice, a bag of frozen mixed vegetables, a handful of barley and some spices. He brought it to a boil, then turned it down to simmer.

By the time he returned, the soup was ready to eat.

He waited, ignoring his growling stomach, hoping Lisa would come downstairs on her own.

She didn't.

Adam waited patiently for another hour before gathering his courage to try to talk to her again. He hated to intrude on her privacy, yet he had to make sure she was okay. He wouldn't forgive himself if he didn't. He tapped his knuckles on the pine door. "Lisa?"

She felt her heart beat faster at the mere sound of Adam's voice. As if his kiss hadn't confused her enough, his apology and her conflicting emotions had totally wiped her out. What could she possibly say now to make things return to normal? She couldn't get involved and stay objective.

He knocked again, and Lisa could almost see his callused knuckles rapping on the wood. She glanced in the mirror on her way to answer the door, studying herself disapprovingly. She looked like a bedraggled waif. She'd skipped her makeup and put on her warmest clothes—a turtleneck, flannel shirt and her only remaining pair of clean blue jeans. If the man was looking for romance, he'd be sorely disappointed.

She took a deep breath, then opened the door. As much as she tried to look him in the eye, she couldn't. She couldn't take the chance that he might see how his kiss had truly affected her. "Hi."

He took a step back, quickly perusing her from head to toe. "Are you okay?"

She nodded.

"I can't tell you how sorry I am."

If he apologized once more, she'd scream. As if it wasn't humiliating enough to have fallen into a pond, melted willingly into his embrace *and* returned his kiss, it was doubly embarrassing to have him take everything back by saying he was sorry he'd kissed her in the first place.

"I shouldn't have yelled at you like that," he said, his voice low and husky. He looked away, then added, "You risked your own safety for Toby, and all I could do was yell. It scared me, seeing you dive into an iced-over pond for a dog."

"What did you expect me to do? Let him drown?"

Adam shrugged like a frightened little boy who'd done something wrong. "I don't know, but I didn't expect you to risk your own life for him." His voice was soft and husky and slathered with honesty. "I didn't come here to argue. I came to thank you...."

She took a step back, her hand automatically reaching up to close the door. "Then you're welcome."

"Wait." He put his hand up to stop the door from closing in his face. "I've made a pot of soup. Why don't you come down and have some?"

"I think you were right, Adam. My coming here was some twist of fate, but staying would be a mistake."

His gaze darted to hers immediately, a look of regret in his brown eyes. "I'm sorry I've made you so miserable. You have every right to want to leave and skip this article altogether. That's fine. I can understand your anger, but I'd like to clear things up, if you're willing to give me another chance.''

She simply stared at him. ''You don't care about the article?'' How could anyone not care about national exposure for their brand-new business? Looking around the lodge, her envy reared to life. It was obviously much easier to toss such an opportunity aside when he had already fulfilled all of his dreams.

Adam shook his head. ''Not really. Right now I'm hungry and you probably are, too. You came for a story and I owe you that much. If you still want it, I'd like to show you around the ranch tomorrow, so you won't hurt yourself. I should have done it long ago, not left it to my sister.''

She didn't miss the fact that he'd not mentioned the kiss directly. Had he only been apologizing for yelling at her? She looked away, too frightened to think about that now. ''What about the article?'' Lisa blinked, then looked him in the eye. ''The editor won't budge. It has to focus on the romantic getaway theme.''

What she saw caught her off guard, and she quickly looked away. The anger and cockiness was gone, replaced by a tenderness she didn't dare acknowledge. He tucked his fingers into the pockets of his black jeans. Adam had changed into a gray T-shirt and a black-and-white-plaid shirt that brought out the strength of his jaw—a strength that had all but disappeared with the gentleness of his kiss.

"Personally, I don't understand what all this fuss is over, but if you want to write a story about the ranch, I guess it's okay. Why don't you come downstairs and we can talk about it?" Was the invitation she heard in his voice limited to dinner and the article, or was there more to it than business?

She started to close the door to her suite, then paused. "Should I bring my notebook?"

"Not tonight. Let's just talk." Keeping an exaggerated distance between them, Adam motioned for her to go ahead.

She gave him a puzzled glance. "Did I do something else wrong?"

He gave her a curt shrug. "I thought you might prefer some space."

She paused. If she was wise, she'd let the subject drop. "Had you apologized for the kiss, I would agree." She held her breath and turned to him. "Did that apology cover kissing me, too?"

His gaze caressed her lips. "Not exactly."

She let out the breath and took another, then told her heart to start beating again. Inside she was smiling, but externally, she wasn't so confident. She was terrified. What was she doing, flirting with a man whose life was the complete opposite of hers? Despite the warning her brain sent, her mouth acted all on its own. "Not exactly?"

He smiled. "Can't say I'm sorry, but I realize it

probably wasn't the wisest thing I've ever done. Now before I'm tempted to complicate business even more, why don't we go eat? I think we've both had enough to test our patience today.''

Maintaining the distance between them became awkward as they both took a step, then jumped back as if electrocuted. ''This is ridiculous, Adam. Don't you care to know if I'm sorry?''

He stared at the floor. ''Not exactly.''

She laughed. ''Why's that?''

''Guess you could say I'm that much of a coward. If you didn't like it, I'd just as soon not know.''

Lisa felt a load had been lifted from her shoulders. She stepped closer and lifted her lips to his rough cheek and kissed him lightly. ''I couldn't agree more, regarding this matter of business, but after we have that taken care of, I wouldn't mind at all if you gave me another. To celebrate, of course.''

He nodded casually, a smile softening his face. ''And what might we be celebrating?''

''Survival?'' she suggested, surprised to feel a twitch on her own lips. ''Or to a job completed? Or maybe I'll get a permanent job offer,'' she added as they walked side by side to the kitchen. Lisa took two soup mugs from the cupboard. ''The possibilities are endless.''

''A permanent job offer? I thought you enjoyed the footloose and fancy-free life of the roving reporter.''

''It is fun, and I do enjoy it, but sometimes...''

Lisa shook her head as she realized what she'd almost said. "Well, I miss the benefits of a job. You know, the security of health insurance, retirement, a regular paycheck..." she muttered hastily.

He silently offered to pour her a glass of milk. She nodded. "Is that all you miss?"

"It's been fun, but there comes a time when a woman has to have a back-up plan. Don't try to read anything more into it than that." Lisa went on to explain the possible job offer.

"You're trying to tell me you don't miss having a home and..." He stumbled over the words.

"A family." She smiled sympathetically.

"I'm sorry. It's none of my business."

She put her hand up to stop his apology. "Don't get me wrong. This 'offer' is far from my dream job, but it is full-time. If something doesn't come along soon, I'll be flipping burgers."

"Would that be at the local stand?"

"What?"

He shrugged. "Just wondering if you're going to be around a little more often. You know, to see your sisters."

"My sisters?" She raised her eyebrows and set her spoon in the soup. "You kiss me like there's no tomorrow and ask me if I'm coming back to visit my sisters?" She shook her head. "We're two mature adults, Adam. There's nothing wrong in enjoying a kiss, is there?"

"That depends."

"On what?"

"On whether the feelings are mutual. Otherwise, I acted out of turn."

She stared at him in silence.

"If that's your answer, then I'd say we'd better keep the relationship strictly business."

"Can't we enjoy a kiss without it *meaning* something? I care about you, Adam, b-but—" she stammered "—it doesn't mean I'm going to demand a commitment. It was only a kiss, for heaven's sake."

He chuckled softly, rubbing his thumb and index finger along his lower lip. "I suppose you're right. After all, your life is on the road, right? And you don't want any ties to slow you down. Is that what you're saying?"

Lisa felt the heat creep up her neck and into her cheeks. Was that what she'd said? "I didn't say that." She shook her head. "Yes, I'll be going sometime, but I'm not leaving yet. In fact," she said, "I was wondering…" Lisa had at least a dozen things going through her head right now, and not one complete sentence in the batch. It was only a kiss. She struggled to put the right question into words. "Actually, I was thinking…about the grand opening." She forced her mind back to the article. Maybe Adam was right after all; mixing business with pleasure was a really bad idea.

"What about it?"

"It seems the least I could do is to help you get ready, since you've agreed to do this article. And I could take the pictures at the celebration. I don't want to add stress by rushing you to get ready."

Adam shook his finger. "My sister put you up to this, didn't she?" He began laughing. "I should have known better...."

Lisa leaned across the table and touched his lips with her finger. "This has nothing to do with your sister, Adam." She felt like she was going to faint; the blood was pumping so fast, it was bypassing her brain. "I hope I don't regret this, but it's kind of peaceful here. I'd like to stay a while longer."

"A while longer?"

"I'll have to leave, eventually. Duty calls. You understand that, don't you?"

What was she saying? What was she asking?

"No commitments. No promises. No regrets."

He had to be crazy to consider her offer. And even crazier to agree. Yet agree he did. Knowing very well that the time would come when he would have to tell her goodbye and hate both of them for this moment. He leaned forward, drawing her closer at the same time. Her hair was silky and soft against his rough hands. *No commitments, no promises, no regrets.* Adam forced himself to keep the kiss short and sweet. "I'm glad you're staying."

To his relief, Lisa smiled demurely and sat back down in the chair across the table and continued the conversation as if nothing momentous had just happened. "Remember, I'm here to help you get ready.

I'm no longer a guest. Agreed? Oh! And not a word to anyone. No brothers or sisters. No one.''

"You keep changing the rules. I may have to reconsider." Maybe nothing had changed. Maybe he was the only one of the two of them that felt the difference. Maybe he was the only one headed toward heartbreak.

He didn't think so. He longed for more smiles like the ones she'd brought into his daily existence in two short days. She'd touched a spark of light to the cobwebs of his past, giving him hope for the future.

Father, help both Lisa and I keep our agreement. Don't let either of us regret the decision we've just made.

Chapter Eleven

Lisa couldn't remember a more pleasant dinner with any man. They lingered over their meal, discussing the history of Whispering Pines.

She asked questions and listened intently while Adam went into detail about wanting to share his grandparents' legacy with others.

Lisa saw his gaze go beyond the timber walls surrounding them. Adam's baritone voice sounded softer than usual. "There's something to be said for listening to the wind whispering through the trees, feeling the sun on your face, losing track of time…"

"I noticed a Bible verse on the desk." She paused, trying to remember the words. "'Come away by yourselves…'"

Silence.

"'…to a lonely place and rest a while.' It's from the book of Mark," Adam finished the quote.

"I take it that's your motto?"

Adam nodded. "Grandpa wasn't doing well and had to be moved into a nursing home. Mom couldn't run the ranch alone. I came to help out."

"What about the rest of the family? Couldn't they help?"

"Alex was wandering the countryside jumping out of airplanes fighting fires, Kevin was spending fourteen hours a day trying to get his own company back on track and my sisters' husbands knew nothing about ranching." Adam shrugged. "I didn't really plan to stay, but in the meantime, God showed me another option."

"You left your career to help your mom?"

Adam got quiet. "It was a good time to make a change."

Lisa stared at him in disbelief. "With no back-up plan, or job security or..."

"Promise?" Adam's eyes met hers, and a look of satisfaction told her she'd been set up. "I was beyond expecting promises of any kind. My integrity had been ripped apart and pieced back together like a jigsaw puzzle by then. All I wanted was to be alone."

She felt her mouth go dry. "I didn't realize. I'm sorry, Adam." She longed to dig deeper, yet not at the expense of causing Adam more pain. If he wanted to tell her what happened, he would.

His smile was warm and tender. "There's nothing to be sorry for. God had a different plan."

He made his faith sound so easy. She had trouble believing people and things she could see, let alone a spiritual being as obscure as God.

Adam could almost see ideas spinning in her mind as she jotted down notes on the paper napkin.

He stretched to see what she was writing.

She smiled. "I agreed to let you give final approval. That doesn't count editorial input during the writing. Don't you trust me?" She tucked the napkin into the hip pocket of her denim jeans and cleared her dishes.

"Just curious."

"Not to worry. You and your land will shine. Now all I need is your help with the pictures." Her pink lips formed a wide smile. "Please."

He shook his head. "I'd hate to break the camera."

"It wasn't you, trust me."

"It's broken?"

"I don't know for certain. I'm afraid it got wet when I fell into the pond. I assume there's a camera store in Fort Collins, isn't there?"

"We can see." Adam pulled the phone book from the drawer of the roll-top desk and thumbed through the business section. "Here's one. Says they sell and repair professional equipment."

"Could you drive me, or should I call a cab?"

Adam laughed out loud. "In this snow, you couldn't get a soul to come out this far." He snapped the book closed. "I can take you tomorrow. I have a few errands to run in town anyway. As you probably noticed on the tour yesterday, I haven't picked up any linens. Would you mind helping me do some shopping?''

"That's our agreement, isn't it?''

By the time they made it into town and found the camera shop, it was late morning, and the place was closed for lunch. "Why don't we run your errands first?'' Lisa turned to face him.

"The bedding store is on the other side of town.'' He pulled the sleeve of his nylon parka aside and checked his watch. "According to the sign, they'll be open in forty minutes. Why don't we browse? Maybe you could help me with some decorating ideas? My sisters have threatened to take matters into their own hands if I don't get it done soon.''

"My, my, we've had a change of heart, haven't we?'' Lisa tucked the camera back into the bag and followed him.

"I may be bullheaded, but I'm not an idiot.''

She laughed. They passed a kitchen store in silence. Then an art gallery displaying Southwestern drawings. Pointing to one, she said, "That would look nice in the great room. Don't you think?''

He studied it then shrugged. "It's nice, but...''

"Not really you, I guess.'' Lisa started walking again. "Maybe...''

"Remember, I'm not in the market for another interior decorator, Lisa. I just thought we could find a few little knickknacks. I repeat, few. I'm not hiring a huge staff—and I'm not fond of dusting.''

His warning didn't seem to faze her as she picked up her pace. "Look at this." Without pause, she pushed the heavy oak door open into a rustic shop.

He had to agree with her. Why had Celeste come in dragging modern art sculptures of wildlife and poorly made replicas of antique furniture when this stuff was available?

"Oh, Adam. Isn't this adorable?''

He looked at Lisa standing next to the whimsical bear carved from a tree stump. She held up the sign that said Out To Lunch on one side and Welcome on the other. Adam smiled. "Cute as can be."

She spun around, hands on her hips. "Are you making fun of me?''

Adam shook his head. I wasn't talking about the bear, sweetheart. He lifted the statue from the display. "I suppose you want me to put the little critter on the deck?''

Lisa stepped back to assess the bear. "He's too small. Maybe the artist could make you a larger version." She cocked her head and smiled. "It could say Feeding the Herds instead of Out To Lunch.''

He returned the bear to the display and gently placed his hand on her back to move her along before she had a ten-foot statue on his bill. "I'll think about it.''

"You really like the idea?'' She looked up to him with those curious eyes of hers.

His heartbeat quickened and a primitive warning sounded in his brain. Lisa looked oddly fragile as she waited for his approval, and he didn't have the heart to let her down. "Yeah, he's okay."

Satisfaction washed over her, and she moved through the store more at ease than he'd seen her since her arrival. She picked up a replica of a rustic old barn lantern and a copper candle holder with a cutout of the silhouette of a pine tree. "I think these would add dimension to the coffee table by the big-screen television."

"Dimension?"

"You know, contrast. Tie the old and the new together. Besides, they'd add an aspect of light to that side of the great room. If someone's watching TV, their back is to the woodstove. Not only that, candles are homey."

Before he knew it, he'd agreed to buy them, and several other items. She disappeared when he went to the proprietor's office to order the special sign for the bear carving.

When she returned, Lisa had a bag of her own which equalled his in size.

"What did you get?"

She smiled, lifting her eyebrows. "Just a couple of gifts. Alissa and Ricky have birthdays coming up."

"Oh, yeah. Guess I'd better do some shopping, too." Adam locked the bags in the truck before they returned to the camera store. Lisa pulled her camera from the bag and handed it to the technician and explained what had happened. She waited silently for his assessment.

The white-haired gentleman glanced up at her, then across the store to Adam. ''I don't see any real damage,'' the man said. ''But I can take a look at it and give you a call tomorrow. First I'll see how this roll of film turns out. Gets kind of pricey replacing a professional setup like this, I suppose you know.''

From the corner of his eye, Adam saw the worry in her expression. ''Yes, I know,'' she all but whispered. ''I'll call tomorrow.''

Adam set the book back on the shelf and stepped up beside her. ''Can I do anything?''

She simply shook her head in silence and headed toward the door.

''Why don't we get a bite to eat?''

''Eat?'' Lisa's hand flew to her mouth. ''Oh, no. I forgot to give you a message last night. A woman called to confirm a lunch date.'' She dragged Adam out the door. ''Oh, drat, I forgot her name.''

Adam glanced at his watch and chuckled. ''It's not like I have a dozen women on a string. Come on, we may as well see if Tara's still there.''

''You're kidding, right? I don't think the woman will appreciate making this a threesome.'' They both climbed into the truck and Adam started the engine.

He turned quickly and looked at Lisa, humored by her reaction. If he didn't know better, he'd say Lisa was jealous. "You didn't think she's my girlfriend—did you?"

Lisa shrugged, a tinge of pink staining her cheeks. "She sounded…well…a bit possessive, like a girlfriend might."

She does care. "And how would a jealous girlfriend sound?"

Lisa buckled her seat belt and hugged her bags to her body. "She kept asking who I was."

Trying to keep the humor from his expression, he said, "And what did you tell her?"

"She asked if I was Millie, I said no. She asked if I was your sister, I said no. I was very professional. I asked for her name and number to take a message for you."

A laugh rumbled from deep in his chest and he leaned across the seat and gave her a quick kiss on the cheek. "Bless you, Lisa. I owe you my life."

Lisa's fingers lingered on the spot he'd just kissed. "You and she aren't…"

He shook his head as he backed out of the parking space and pressed the accelerator. "Let me make one thing absolutely clear right now. I don't kiss one woman while I'm dating, seeing or in any way involved with another. Not that Tara wouldn't love to claim otherwise. She's on the Sweetheart Festival committee." On the way to the restaurant, Adam explained how Tara had weaseled her way on to the site selection committee and into the position as hostess. As he pulled into a parking place at the Italian restaurant, Adam added, ''Whatever you do, don't make the lady mad. The last thing I need right now is to have her leave me to host this thing myself.''

Chapter Twelve

"**H**i, I'm sorry we're late." Adam realized his mistake when he saw the shock on Tara's face turn to fury. Tara's skin flushed all the way down to her generously exposed cleavage.

He'd had to drag Lisa out of the truck and into the restaurant, assuring her the entire way that there never was, nor had there ever been anything between him and the woman who had affixed herself to the idea that there was a romance brewing.

Adam held Lisa's chair for her, then casually pulled an extra chair from a nearby table for himself. Through the tight-lipped smile, Tara's tone was velvet, yet edged with steel daggers. "Adam, I didn't realize you were bringing anyone. Is she one of your hired help for the party?"

Apparently there had been more to Lisa and Tara's conversation than simply words. He laughed lightly, hoping Tara wouldn't read any more into Lisa's presence. "No, Lisa's a family friend who's visiting the ranch for a while. We had errands to run in town this morning and I didn't think it would be hospitable to leave her to find lunch on her own."

Tara deliberately removed the reading glasses from her nose. Her gaze darted between them and settled visciously on Lisa. "I see. I'm surprised you didn't simply say that last night, Lisa."

Lisa glanced at Adam, then to Tara. "Most establishments value a guest's privacy second only to their owner's. I simply answered the phone as a courtesy to Adam."

Adam hoped his smile reflected his appreciation of Lisa's tact. While he didn't want to alienate Tara two weeks before the celebration, he certainly wasn't into fueling her assumption that he shared her interest in the two of them dating.

The three ordered, and Adam turned the conversation to the business at hand. Valentine's Day.

Tara efficiently opened her leather-covered day planner to the Sweetheart Ball header. "I've arranged with the county maintenance crews to grade or plow the roads to the ranch the afternoon of the party. I don't want ruts or snow to stop anyone from attending. We've poured too much into this."

Adam said, "I wouldn't have thought either to be a problem any typical Colorado winter, but with every record from precipitation to low temperatures being broken this year, I wouldn't doubt anything."

He took a drink of water. "You might want to see if you can reserve plows for late that night, as well, in case we get snow during the party. I don't need to find beds for two hundred guests my opening night."

"Nor would we want *anything* to force the committee to back out of the commitment to Whispering Pines at this late date," Tara said in a sultry voice. Tara explained how the celebration had evolved to honor Whispering Pine's historical status in the community. Lisa's quick retort included facts about the ranch even he'd forgotten.

Not to be outdone, Tara tried to counter with another fact, and got it all wrong.

Not missing the subtle threats Tara had tossed into the conversation, Adam interrupted them. "And the caterers are bringing the food out..."

"At four," Tara finished for him, ignoring the young woman refilling their drinks. "I've ordered my gown from the boutique on Columbine, but I'll need your size to order a tux. Would you like me to bring it out for you that morning?"

"I'm sure you'll have enough to do. I'll make the arrangements," he said. He felt as if the temperature in the room had gone up twenty degrees. He could almost hear the innuendo Tara had given Lisa on the phone. If he didn't know better, her remarks could leave people believing he was practically a married man. He shuddered to think it.

He heard Lisa whisper to the waitress and Adam

nodded his thanks to the young lady as she set his plate in front of him, grateful for her prompt service. Tara went through the party hors d'oeuvres menu for at least the fifteenth time. "Did something change since last time we discussed the menu?"

Tara looked back at her notes while Adam took another bite of lasagna. "No, why?"

"I thought I must have missed a change. It sounds like you have everything under control, Tara. I'm sure the event will be a huge success."

Lisa ate her ravioli marinara without meeting his gaze. What in the world must she be thinking?

Tara took a bite of shrimp and linguini. "Lisa," she said with a clump of food in her cheek, "are you planning to stay for the masquerade ball?"

Surprised, Lisa forced her bite down before attempting an answer. "I haven't quite decided yet, but you're making it quite inviting. It sounds like a perfect conclusion..."

Adam nudged her knee with his.

Taking a sip of water, she paused the just long enough to nudge him back. "To my visit," Lisa continued. "I wouldn't miss being here to support such dear friends as the MacIntyres."

Adam couldn't get out of here fast enough. If he didn't, who knew what the two women would come up with next? He asked for their bills, and excused himself and Lisa as soon as she indicated she was ready.

Obviously caught off guard by his quick departure,

Tara hadn't finished eating. "Adam, will next week, same time, work to finalize plans?"

Shaking his head, Adam declined. "I have a lot of last-minute details at the ranch to oversee from here on out. Call if there are changes."

Tara looked at him, then Lisa, with a look of revenge. He moved his hand to Lisa's waist to escort the drifter away from Tara's lethal glare.

He didn't relax until the restaurant doors closed behind them.

It took Lisa all of two seconds to react. "You..." she began, spinning around to scold him.

He lowered his face close to hers. "Deserve every rotten thing you could say about me, but after we're out of her view, please. And try not to look as if *everything* I said was a fabrication. I do still have to work with the woman for two more weeks."

Lisa's smile was one of triumph, pure and simple. She could easily have fed him to the wolves, and right now he couldn't wait to find out why she hadn't.

He unlocked her door and helped her inside. She started to protest again, but he raised his hand to stop her. "Hold that thought."

She buckled up and waited silently until they'd turned onto College Drive. "You are a cad."

"I had that coming."

Lisa's voice rose an octave. "You could have warned me that she would come at me with claws out."

"Wait just a minute. Your phone conversation with Tara should've clued you into that." Adam turned into the shopping center, hoping that setting Lisa free to spend his money would take her mind off his less-than-stellar behavior. "What do you say we buy some bedding?"

Lisa ignored his question. "Why didn't you tell her the truth about why I'm here? And why didn't you tell me your grand opening is a masquerade ball?" she demanded without allowing time to answer either. "It is the perfect conclusion to this story. A masquerade ball on Valentine's Day. My editor will love it."

"Lisa, I'm sorry for putting you in an awkward position with Tara. And I admit, you handled it with incredible class."

She gazed at him with her sweet musing look. "So what was that nudge for?"

Her eyes twinkled with mischief, and he felt trouble brewing. "I wasn't sure what you were going to say. I don't want Tara to find out about the magazine or the article." Suddenly Adam realized he had lost the willpower to push her away. He would let her do this story her way.

Lisa laughed. "Well, you can bet I won't be the one to tell her, but just knowing the woman, your secret isn't safe for long."

She was probably right. And if his past luck with women was any indication, he'd spend the rest of his life picking up the pieces.

They stepped into the department store side by side. Something told him his plans of being home in time for evening chores were shot.

Adam had never seen so much bedding in his life. "One word of warning. No ruffles, no lace, no frills," he said as she pulled a cart from the rack and handed it to him, taking another for herself.

She turned around and looked at him wide-eyed. "Oh, no you don't. If you want my advice, I'm willing to give it, but it's your ranch." She pushed the cart forward, nudging him to take the lead.

"There you go changing the rules again."

She smiled mischievously, "Come on. Picking out bedding isn't painful. It just takes an imagination."

Adam started down the aisle, pulling the cart behind him. He tossed five sets of hunter-green sheets from one shelf—pillowcases from another—into the basket as he walked. He skipped the pink sets and moved on to the blue, then added to the assortment. The last set landed with a splat on the linoleum floor. He turned to find Lisa frantically putting the sheets back on the shelf.

"What are you doing?"

"Trying to save you a few hundred dollars." She pointed at the designer label. "Not to mention, you have to look at the bed size. I don't think you have many twins in the lodge, do you?"

"No, none."

"And dark colors fade. Just a suggestion, I'd stick with the lighter shades for the sheets since they get washed so often. Now, first you need to decide on a color for each room.'' She pulled out her notepad and pen and leaned against the shelves, taking tally of furniture color, size and style.

"We just received the beds a week ago—let's see…'' Adam recited the information from memory.

"Color preferences?''

Adam looked around, then shrugged. "That's why I need your help. And with your traveling experience, you surely have ideas of what works and what doesn't.''

"Why don't we start with the same colors for two or three rooms so you can mix and match if need be?'' She headed toward the hunter green and burgundy first.

Five hours, three stores and he didn't dare add up how many dollars later, they had the bedding, towels and guest room window coverings purchased. The back of the truck was heaped full. He carried the boxes into the lodge, hoping Lisa would hurry and get everything put into the rooms they belonged in before he managed to mix them up.

They worked late into the evening, racing to open packages, removing all the tags and getting the piles of linens into the four industrial-size washers.

The phone rang as the two of them ran through the kitchen each carrying a load of towels. Adam paused to take the call, giving Lisa the chance to ease ahead. "Hello.'' Adam laughed breathlessly into the phone.

"Is Adam there?" Katarina asked hesitantly.

"Kat, this *is* Adam. Who'd you think was answering my phone?"

"It doesn't sound like you." His sister-in-law's voice was thick with concern.

Adam had no doubts that Katarina was serious, and felt a laugh work its way up from deep in his chest. "Don't worry, it's me, and I'm fine. Is everything there okay? Do you want to talk to your sister?"

"Yeah, everything's okay. Your mom and I've been busy getting the nursery ready. Must be the nesting instinct kicking in. Poor Alex can't believe how much stuff it takes to get ready for a baby."

Adam laughed again. "Tell him he's got nothing to complain about. Your sister and I just bought sixty sheets..."

"Sixty-four," Lisa yelled over the sound of water spilling into the stainless-steel tub.

"Correction, sixty-four." He took the cordless phone into the laundry room and handed it to Lisa. "Why don't you talk, and I'll do this?"

He could only imagine the suspicion that would result from Lisa and Katarina's conversation. His family would think he'd absolutely lost his mind, making games out of doing the laundry. And he'd never hear the end of Lisa getting him to accomplish in one afternoon what they had nagged him to do for two months. He had to agree; it was nothing short of a miracle.

While Lisa visited with her sister, she continued to sort bedding into rooms and silently assign each of them a stack to carry up the stairs. How she managed to keep everything straight was a mystery. Next she ripped open the packages of curtains and motioned for him to bring her the ironing board, iron and a spray bottle. Before he returned, she and her sister had finished talking.

He emerged from his house with the ironing equipment. "Where do you want these?"

"Since we're going to hang them upstairs, we may as well work up there. Before we start on that, why don't I fix us a sandwich while you take care of the animals? It's almost nine."

Adam leaned the board against the wall and met her next to the refrigerator. She turned to set the mayonnaise on the counter and he pulled her into his arms. "You made today a lot more fun than work, Lisa. You can't imagine how I've dreaded doing this."

She put her hands around his neck. "Then why didn't you let your mom and sisters take it over?"

"If you saw their frilly bedrooms, you'd understand. And—" he shrugged "—I wanted to do it myself, but I couldn't have done any of it without your help. You have a terrific eye for this sort of thing."

"I was an art major, Adam. Photography and journalism were minors, but there's a lot more money in them right now." Her smile invited him to end the conversation. "Besides," she whispered, "interior decorating is only fun when your taste matches that of the customer."

"Let's test your theory." He closed his eyes and lowered his lips to hers. Adam struggled to keep his feelings for the drifter from going any deeper, but that, too, was quickly getting out of hand. She felt perfect in his embrace. She made the mundane an adventure, and as she herself admitted, their tastes were perfectly matched. What more could a man ask for?

Chapter Thirteen

Lisa glanced at Adam, then quickly diverted her gaze. Sleep had been next to impossible after working all evening with Adam and sharing another of his memory-erasing kisses. This morning, she had to stick to business. Falling in love did not fit into her plan. And falling for Adam—well...she simply couldn't overlook how painful leaving would be.

"So," she said, looking from the lodge to the barn then on to a building beyond the corrals, "you've been spending a lot of time out here. What do you do besides feeding the livestock?"

Adam picked up a stick and threw it. Toby took off across the snow-fluffed pasture. "Work in my shop, refurbishing furniture. You like antiques?"

She nodded. "Have you restored all of the items in the lodge yourself?"

"Most of them. Mom loves garage sales, and I like

returning pieces to their original beauty. I'm not much for this trend of keeping them in a state of disrepair in order to retain the piece's value. Care to see my latest project?''

"Sure." She followed him to the log building next to the barn. He swung open the oversize door, turned on the lights and a loud fan buzzed. The distinct odor of chemicals lingered, though not overwhelmingly so.

The room was neat and orderly, just like the rest of Adam's world. Workbenches and shelves lined the walls and tools were meticulously arranged.

Lisa couldn't help but wonder if Adam kept every aspect of his life in such impeccable order. She followed him across the room, past a variety of power tools. Buckets and coffee cans held miscellaneous brushes and steel wool. She spun around, examining the area. "I must admit, I've never seen anyone quite so organized."

"Scary, huh?" He chuckled. "It's not as bad as it looks. I like things to move smoothly. I have to keep the sanding and wood tools as far from the finishing area as I can so the room stays dustless. The fan helps with that and removing fumes."

Lisa noticed the odor was nearly gone. "This looks pretty professional. Are you doing it just to furnish the lodge or is it another business venture?"

"Haven't decided yet. We have more furniture than we can ever use. You wouldn't believe what all Mom brings home. It's so bad that my sisters, your sisters and even Meg are dragging things home now.''

Lisa grinned. ''I know. Things and people.''

''I didn't mean you, and if...''

Lisa laughed and moved right on to the next question, leading Adam to hand her a mask and take her step-by-step through the refinishing process. He spread chemicals over the painted wood surface and let it set while he took her into the next room and closed the door behind them. ''This is where I apply the finish, so the door has to stay closed.'' Before them stood a clawfoot oak double-pedestal dining room table. ''That way, when I apply the varnish there are no little specks to sand out—well, fewer at least.''

''This is beautiful.'' She stepped forward and examined it closely. Lisa reached for it, stopping herself just before she touched it.

''It's dry. Go ahead,'' he said.

She ran her hand over the satin finish, feeling tiny ridges where the oak grain enhanced the richness of the piece.

''Grandpa's parents brought this with them all the way from Virginia in the late 1800s. I decided it was about time it had a face-lift.''

Lisa couldn't keep from looking up at Adam—to the modest, matter-of-fact, nonassuming way he viewed all of this. He was restoring history, devoting his life to the heritage his forefathers had passed down. He valued family and honor more than anyone she'd ever met. She backed her way to the door and returned to the other room.

"You okay?" Adam's hand touched hers and Lisa nodded.

"What's next?" She moved immediately to the fancy two-drawer dresser and pretended to study it.

The entire drawer front was covered with a pale pink slime. Adam put on gloves and started scraping the muck into a plastic bucket with a flat broad blade tool. "We need to get down through all these layers to the bare wood."

"I can't believe you see hope for this. No offense, but it looks awful." She ran her finger over a blister in the dresser top.

Adam poured solution over the dresser and spread it with the paintbrush. "Give it a week. You won't believe it's the same piece," he said. "I always look at a piece as if it were God looking at me. I sure hope He can see through all the layers and see promise in what I could be, with a little spit and polish."

His analogy burst the questions bubbling in her head. Since she didn't want Adam to ask the same of her, she wouldn't probe any further. He was baiting her, and this time she wouldn't bite.

Adam had cleaned away the slime, which left only bits of color trapped in the grain and the grooves of the carved design on the front of the drawer. He dabbed a bit more solution on those spots then moved back to the dresser top and zipped away the paint.

Lisa moved closer to examine the damage. "Now what do you do with this?" She ran her fingers over the large split in the veneer.

"It just needs a little tender loving care." He took a piece of fine steel wool, dipped it into a small bowl of solution and cleaned away the excess residue, then pulled a large syringe from the cabinet and popped the protective cover off. "I use this livestock syringe to inject wood glue under the veneer." Going all directions, he squeezed the goo into the opening, then picked up a flat board from a pile of scraps. "We cover the wood with a piece of waxed paper in case any glue oozes out...clamp the wood over the bubble and it should take care of the problem. You'll never even notice a scar."

Lisa looked at the piece as if it had been under the care of a skilled surgeon's hand. "Huh." She wondered if Adam always looked at a piece as if it were a patient waiting for analysis.

"And now, we're going to get rid of all this extra crud that has gathered in the crevices." He moved back to the drawer. After clearing the first layers of paint from the deep grooves with a pointed trowel, he took out a dentist's tool and carefully dug in the corners of the finely carved cornices, dabbing extra solution on where excess paint had collected. Like a caterpillar hungrily munching back and forth across the width of a leaf, Adam carefully dug, then dabbed and cleaned some more, until the deep mahogany color of the wood hadn't a trace of pink enamel on it.

"Where did a finance major learn to refinish furniture?"

"Grandpa was always fixing something, and I loved watching. The first time he gave me a nightstand to refinish, I thought it was a lost cause. Ever since then, I've loved the entire process of restoration. And like the dining room table, I love seeing the results and knowing that someone will be enjoying the same pieces that others have enjoyed for decades. It disturbs me to see the waste—like old buildings left to rot and decay against the harsh elements."

Lisa could see the passion in his eyes. It wasn't just this ranch that meant so much to him, it was all of it—the history as well as his heritage. This land was as much a part of Adam MacIntyre as those irresistible brown eyes or his sun-streaked hair. Separating the two would prove catastrophic to both.

Adam spent the remainder of the afternoon giving Lisa the grand tour of the ranch. Toby lumbered along beside them. He'd given Lisa a choice of horseback or snowshoes, and to his surprise, she'd chosen the latter. "You're a natural," Adam said as she passed him by.

She tossed her hair over her shoulder. "Must be the patience of the instructor. Either that, or he's still feeling guilty."

Adam laughed. "Not a chance." He was living

dangerously, letting his guard down with her. It was more than the guilt, and he knew it now. He picked up a handful of snow, formed it into a ball and threw it toward the ponderosa pines. Toby shot across the meadow after it and they both watched in silence.

Minutes later Adam said, "I enjoyed today."

"I did, too. Thank you." She stopped and took a deep breath. "I can see why you love it here."

Could she really understand that this land was as vital to his life as the blood in his veins? "I'll do whatever it takes to keep hold of Whispering Pines."

"Once we get this article out there, you'll have no problem finding customers. Now you have to promise to bring me out again sometime to get pictures."

He stopped next to her. "I didn't think you believed in promises."

"Slip of the tongue."

He leaned close. "I do promise to bring you out again and again. It's about time you realize, Lisa, that not everyone breaks their promises. I'm a man of my word." His gaze dropped to her lips. Fear glimmered in her eyes. Lisa draped her arms across the top rail of the corrals and rested her chin on her hands. "Could I go along while you do chores this evening?"

"Don't you ever slow down?"

Lisa tilted her head to look him. "Nothing to slow down for."

"Ever stop to think you might find something worth slowing down for if you looked for it?"

' She was silent. Adam stood next to her and tried to imagine what she was seeing. She didn't respond. "It took hitting rock bottom to figure out I wasn't where I needed to be," he said gently.

"Well, I've already been there, and I survived."

Adam waited, hoping she'd continue. "What happened to that boyfriend you had last year?"

The wind whispered through the forest.

"He took a hike," she finally admitted.

"Painful, huh?"

"Not in the way you're thinking, it wasn't. Men like him are a dime a dozen." Her entire face turned pink, confirming she was genuinely embarrassed by her jibe. "I didn't mean all men are a dime a dozen." Her gloved hands flew to her face. "Oh," she groaned. "Me and my big mouth. Adam, I meant nothing personal by that. And I don't have…I mean, I haven't had another boyfriend since Dale. I just meant…"

She was totally flustered, and Adam found her embarrassment almost charming, other than the fact that she was miserable.

"You know," she retorted, "if you weren't such a cad, you would break in here anytime now."

Adam cocked his head to one side. "Kind of difficult to follow a statement like that, being a cad and all."

Her blush spread. "I'm never saying another word."

He smiled. "Promises, promises."

Lisa picked up a handful of snow from the fence post and tossed it at him. "He was the scum of the earth. Being a cad is a compliment compared to him."

"Great. Now you're actually comparing me to the scum of the earth. Save me here. What did the man do that was so terrible?"

Lisa shook her head. "I don't talk about it, to anyone. But all joking aside—he's nowhere in the same league as you."

"All due respect, Lisa, you don't open a door like that and expect a man not to want a few details. You've got the wheels-a-turning, and I don't like the ideas I'm generating." He wanted to think she trusted him enough to clarify her feelings. And he didn't even want to think what could have possibly caused her enough pain to make such a statement about the entire male gender.

She squeezed her eyes closed and took a deep breath.

"Would you rather I ask your sisters?"

Lisa shook her head. "They don't know any of it."

"You've gone through this alone? You haven't told anyone?" Adam took a deep breath and felt the crisp, cold air burn his sinuses.

Again she shook her head. She removed her gloves and frantically wiped tears away. "Why did you have to bring this up?" Lisa pulled her gloves back on and pushed past him.

Adam raised his hands and shrugged his shoulders. "All I wanted to know is if you're seeing anyone. You're the one who said that all men are jerks."

She nearly fell as she turned around. "I never said that."

"You may as well have. And you still haven't answered my question. You come here and think you're the only one who can do the asking?" She didn't respond. "You're not the only person on earth who's been hurt, you know."

Lisa placed her hands on her hips. "Just forget I said anything. I didn't ask you to tell me all about your love life. In fact, I couldn't care less."

He knew better. "Any journalist would want to know all the details, and the juicier the better."

"Then I guess I'm not that kind of journalist."

"You don't want to know that I was being considered for partner with the investment firm I worked for? Or that my girlfriend was getting information from my files and sending it on to investors?"

As she listened to him recount the details of the probing attack against his character and ethics, a look of silent understanding crossed the distance between them. "No, I don't. You don't have to tell me this."

"What? You're out of questions?"

He'd struck a chord.

A look of withdrawal darkened her eyes. "Why are you telling me this, Adam?"

He weighed her with a critical squint and a momentary look of discomfort crossed her face. "I want you to know I understand what it's like to be betrayed. I know what it's like to lose trust in the opposite sex, someone you cared about, trusted, even thought you loved. After months of interrogation, every aspect of my life was picked apart like someone trying to find a needle in a haystack. I came here to catch up with myself and figure out what I really wanted when all of it was over. I found it all right here.''

''You said you left your job to help your mom. You didn't say you were fired.''

''I was suspended during the investigation, and after it was over they 'generously' offered me my same position as junior executive. When the investigation started, I was sure that another chance was what I wanted, but once I came home, going back didn't matter.''

''And your girlfriend?'' He sensed that it wasn't the journalist in Lisa asking the question this time.

''She went to prison.''

Lisa started back to the lodge. Adam followed. A few minutes later, her soft voice broke the silence. ''At least justice was served, Adam. And on top of that, you ended up here. Not bad for a second choice.''

''Sometimes, we're so set in reaching that goal that we can't see what God has planned for us elsewhere. I thought a career in finance was exactly what I wanted. If Amelia hadn't betrayed me, I may have never understood God's plan.''

They reached the lodge and Lisa bent down to unlace her snowshoes. "Not everyone has something like Whispering Pines to fall back to."

"No," he said softly, "but everyone has choices, if they're willing to take a chance now and then."

"You don't have a clue what you're talking about. You haven't any idea who I am or where I've been."

"I see a woman who's afraid to slow down long enough to fill the emptiness with anything of true meaning. Tell me, Lisa, what's important to you?"

She stared at him with a blank expression. Fear dimmed her face. "Same as everyone, I suppose." She shrugged. "A job, money, family, I guess."

Adam tried to hide his disappointment. "You guess? You need to know what's important before you can find peace."

Chapter Fourteen

Lisa hung up the phone. She took a deep breath and released it. One, two, three… "There's no way, Steve. I won't do that to Adam." She and the magazine editor had gone back and forth for three days about the story—ever since she'd told them about the Sweetheart Festival. Now the pressure was on. Lisa wondered if she was right for this business after all.

Maybe Adam was right. Maybe it was time for her to look for another career, to really find out what was important to her. First there were problems with the camera, then the chromes weren't exactly what they were looking for and the story wasn't "captivating" enough. She never should have sent Francie the roll of film with Adam on it.

"Toby, want to go for a walk?"

"Woof." He ran to the door, his tail wagging nonstop, and waited eagerly for Lisa to put her coat on.

She looked outside at the freshly fallen snow and added a pair of wool socks before she put her boots on. Taking a piece of paper from Adam's desk, she wrote, "Taking Toby for a walk. See you for lunch. Lisa." She left it where he'd be sure to see it.

After three steps, Lisa realized her walk would have to be taken on snowshoes. She went to the shed and found the pair she'd worn the last time. She pulled her hood over her fleece headband and tightened the drawstring, put her gloves back on and headed for the pasture.

The brisk air was refreshing. She let it fill her head, her lungs, her mind. Unfortunately, it wasn't enough to block out the disagreement she'd had with Steve this morning or the niggling feeling that her career was over.

She didn't want to face Adam. She didn't want to hurt him now, after she'd worked so hard to gain his trust. Why had she even mentioned the festival? It wasn't like Whispering Pines would be featuring romantic galas every weekend. Her brilliant idea was about to backfire.

Lisa watched Toby root through the snow, as if looking for a bone he'd buried for dessert. She made a snowball. "Toby, fetch." She threw the ball and watched absently as the dog ran to find it.

She'd never gone against an editor's orders, not even when she'd felt the story would be better from another angle. What had changed?

Adam.

Because of him, she'd broken every professional rule in the book. She had gotten too involved. She'd put her feelings for him before the assignment, and now more than ever, she couldn't afford the distraction of a romantic interlude.

Lisa erased everything from her mind except the article, mentally exploring ideas to make everyone happy. Time slipped away as Lisa pondered the events of the past two weeks.

Toby, who had bounced along next to her while she struggled with each step, was now nowhere to be found. Adam had warned her not to wait until she was tired to turn around, as she'd still have that same distance to get home. Everywhere she looked, it was white. Taking tiny steps, she turned and looked for the lodge.

It's gone. In every direction, Lisa found a curtain of snow blocking the view. How did a mansion like that just disappear?

"Toby?" She felt a moment of panic. "Toby, come," Lisa said, repeating the command properly.

He darted out of nowhere as if he'd never been happier. Probably hadn't been, she guessed. He'd probably never seen so much snow. Lisa bent over and hugged Toby. "You scared me." She looked into his soft brown eyes. "You wouldn't happen to know the way home, would you?"

In the distance she could make out a dark line which she guessed to be trees. She reasoned that the woods were just above the lodge at some point, and she'd be wise to find, then follow them. Eventually she'd see the red roof. Her feet felt like weights as she approached the trees, sinking into the drifts.

She dragged in a deep breath and tears welled in her eyes. Not only had she lost her way in life, she was lost in a snowstorm. Adam had proclaimed that God was to credit for helping him find his way home. Despite their many talks in the past few days, Adam didn't understand. He made it sound so simple.

Where had God been during this past year when she'd needed direction more than ever? Why hadn't He helped her through? She recalled the e-mail Emily had sent her about the footprints in the sand.

Lisa looked behind her. There were no tracks from her snowshoes. She took another step and watched it disappear before her eyes. Panic snapped her last fragile strand of control.

"Adam!" She screamed repeatedly at the top of her lungs until her voice disappeared altogether. *God, if You're really out there taking care of me, let Adam find us.* She trudged on, tired, cold and hungry. It had to be past lunchtime. Surely Adam had found her note by now. He'd come looking for her soon.

Lisa paused to catch her breath and an icy gust knocked her down. She stood, fearful images building in her mind. She moved into the trees for protection from the wind. As she stepped over a downed tree, she twisted her ankle and landed flat on her back. She lay still for a moment then looked behind her at a rocky cliff. *I don't remember anything like* that when Adam showed me the ranch. Trying to get up, she slipped again and banged her knee on the sharp edge of a boulder. Toby ran up beside her and licked her face. His warm tongue only served to warn her how cold she was. "Thanks, boy." She unfolded the tube of her turtleneck over her cheeks and nose, then tried again to stand. Every time she tried to put her hands down, they sank eight inches into the ground. "Come here, Toby." The dog paused. "Toby, come."

Lisa took hold of Toby, and he darted, slipping from her grasp. A soft groan escaped. She looked around. Everything was white. There wasn't even a shadow of a dog to comfort her. She scooted close to the rocks and struggled to her feet. Pain shot up her leg and she crumbled to the ground.

"Snow flurries... The weather forecast said nothing about a blizzard," she whispered. Lisa straightened her leg and the pain intensified. She choked back a cry, frightened to think of the odds of anyone finding her in this storm.

"First step in survival—keep thinking. Two—if you can't find your way out, stay put." She swallowed, trying to soothe her raspy voice. "Even hearing Adam yell at me would be a treat right now."

Find what's important to you... Lisa's breath turned ragged. "Adam..."

Wind blew the snow, not only on the way down, but whipped it up from the ground and swirled it into mounds. Ignoring the pain, she pulled her legs close, afraid to take the snowshoes off for fear she couldn't get them back on if she had to try walking out again. Curling into a ball, Lisa wrapped her arms around her legs and tucked her face next to her knees to protect herself from the wind.

It was easy to understand where Adam's grandparents had come up with the name Whispering Pines. She wished the trees would simply whisper, because right now they howled, creaked and whistled an eerie tune. She puckered her lips and blew. Nothing came out. She was tired and thirsty.

"Don't go to sleep, Lisa," she whispered, then took a handful of snow and put it into her mouth. The cool moisture eased the pain so much, she took another. She moved her fingers. Even with ski gloves on, they were beginning to tingle. Her toes were numb.

"Think. What was that alpine survival guide's name? Mike...Mitch?" It didn't matter, she knew, but the information in the article she'd written for the backpacker magazine could save her life. "Matt?"

Concentrating on names that started with the letter *M* might keep her awake anyway. She had to have a distraction.

"Mark. His name was Mark." She smiled with satisfaction. "Mark...something."

Never mind. Remember the article.

She envisioned the sidebar. "One. Pray."

She'd thought Mark was joking. He didn't seem

to fit the churchy type. Mark spent his weekends outdoors as a guide. Cross-country skiing, hiking, rock climbing, snowmobiling—didn't matter, Mark did it. When did a guy like him have time for God?

Pray.

Lisa lifted her face from the shelter of her arms. The sky was darker. Her heart beat faster. It was harder to breathe. Her rear end felt as if she'd sat in a prickly cactus patch. She looked at her feet. *Who am I kidding? I won't be walking out.* The snowshoes were useless on her feet, but maybe they'd keep her from getting so wet. She unlaced each one and scooted them under her bottom.

She pulled her hands into the arms of her coat and stretched her back. "Adam. Hel-l-l-p!" She listened for a reply.

Just the trees whispering. Gusts calmed to a soft stillness, but the icy breeze stung her eyes.

Where was she? She still couldn't see the lodge.

What's important to you?

She lowered her face to her knees, ignoring her initial glib responses—money, security, a job. What had happened to her?

Pray.

Tears froze in the corner of her eyes.

You probably aren't listening, God. Lisa looked up to the gray ceiling hovering above, then quickly lowered her face to the protection again. *Remember me, little Lisa from Nebraska? You remember, the one who wanted her daddy to come home.*

Tears warmed a path down her cheeks and dripped onto her legs.

He never came. Lisa took a deep breath and her body relaxed momentarily. *You stopped listening. But in case You're still there...*

Lisa's eyes drifted closed and she jerked awake. *Never mind, God. It's too late anyway.*

Her stomach growled. *My sisters say You still care— I don't know about that. I'm still homeless...* She paused midthought. *Kind of homeless—I always had a roof...* Her eyelids felt as if they were glued shut and her mind ran through the fourteen months she'd spent wandering the country.

Lisa recalled the words of the poem. ''It was then that I carried you...''

It was you, God? You were listening?

Lisa awoke to Toby's cold nose nudging between her face and her arms. ''Toby,'' she slurred. ''Toby, where's Adam? Did you bring Adam?''

''I'm right here.'' His voice seemed miles away. She looked up as he dismounted the huge animal before her. Toby barked in her ear.

''I'm lost,'' she said in a soft raspy whisper.

Adam knelt next to her. ''I noticed. This storm caught everyone off guard.'' He moved the fabric from Lisa's face and examined her, then pulled the turtleneck over her nose again. ''You look pretty good, considering. I'm going to get you home and warmed up.''

She gazed into his eyes, surprised to find him watching her.

His eyes turned misty.

Must be the wind.

Adam blinked. "Any tingling—legs, arms, fingers, toes?"

Lisa stretched her legs in front of her and winced, then pushed her hands out of her coat sleeves. "My fingers started to, but they're better now. I twisted my ankle. I can't feel my feet."

"Your legs feel okay?"

Her breathing was slow and labored. "Cold. Very cold."

He nodded. "You did a good job protecting yourself." Adam eased closer. "I'm going to help you up. Think you can pull yourself onto the saddle?"

One glance at the horse, and she knew the answer. She shook her head. "No...no way."

"It's okay. I'll pull you up with me."

Again she looked at the distance from the ground to the saddle, and shrugged. "Yeah...right," she slurred.

"Don't sound so skeptical. You'll be fine." Adam helped her to her feet, grabbed the snowshoes and called the horse closer, still offering her support. "Hold on a minute." Adam turned, staying close enough for her to lean on.

"Toby, come. Sit." Adam tied the snowshoes onto Toby's blue backpack. "Good boy." Toby barked.

Lisa glanced at Toby, blinked, then looked back at the dog again. "He's a...a rescue dog?"

"We're training for the local search-and-rescue team."

Lisa longed to collapse again. She was tired and sore—beyond feeling the cold. She smiled weakly. "Lucky me."

Adam eased her closer to the horse, then put his foot in the stirrup and swung his leg over the animal's back, seating himself behind the saddle. He leaned down and pulled her into the leather seat in front of him. "Come on, sweetie. Swing your leg over. We'll be home in a few minutes."

Seconds later she was settled on the horse's back with Adam's arm around her. As if by magic, he pulled a blanket out of somewhere, covered her legs and tucked it behind her knees.

Adam made a clicking sound with his tongue and slapped the reins against the horse's neck. "Let's head home, Thunder."

Chapter Fifteen

Adam pulled the brim of his grandfather's Stetson low over his eyes, blocking the wind. He hadn't seen this much snow in the last two winters combined. Radio announcers were calling it the blizzard of the decade. A foot had fallen in the past eight hours—a rare occurrence at Whispering Pines.

Thunder ducked his head against the wind and plowed through the heavy snow. Adam looked down at Toby, trotting along beside them with determination.

Lisa's head bobbed. Probably tired, he decided. She'd been out less than five hours, yet from the distance she'd covered, she must have been moving most of the time. "Lean back, Lisa. I have you." He eased her head to rest in the crook of his neck and tipped his hat close to protect her face from the wind.

While they were still experiencing white-out conditions, actual temperatures hadn't dropped much below freezing. Still, gusts kept the chill factor plenty dangerous. Forecasters didn't look for the storm to move out for another twenty-four hours.

The lodge looked dark as they approached. It could be a cold night without electricity. Adam rode up to the back door and dismounted, holding Lisa tight with one hand. He pulled her into his arms, opened the door, then rushed inside.

Adam laid her on the couch in front of the woodstove. He eased her hood back and gently pulled the turtleneck from her face. "I'll be right back, Lisa. I need to put Thunder in the barn." She snuggled into the sofa and closed her eyes.

Adam hurried through unsaddling Thunder and made sure the animals had enough water and feed to last the night.

As he entered the lodge, Adam tossed his coat into the corner and found the matches. He lit the oil lamp on the kitchen wall, took it into the next room and lit all the candles, making a mental note to fill the cupboard with emergency supplies.

He picked up the phone to call Emily, hoping to confirm treatment for Lisa's possible frostbite. Though he'd handled mild cases of his own, dealing with someone else was a totally different issue. The phone was dead. "Well, God, looks like it's You and me."

Adam looked at Lisa, sound asleep. He would never in his life be able to erase the memory of her curled into a ball, covered with an inch of snow. The soft glow of the fire illuminated her fragile features. He had to get her out of those wet clothes.

He added another log to the fire. With the high-beamed ceilings, there was little hope of staying warm in here. Even with the catalytic converter on the stove to crank up the heat, it wouldn't take long before all of the heat rose to the second floor.

"Lisa, wake up." Her puffy eyelids reluctantly parted. Adam pulled her hands from under her head and carefully removed the wet gloves. He unzipped her parka and slipped it off, then gently tugged the thick fleece headband from her ears. Her body let out an involuntary shudder as she woke.

She had gone out well prepared for the elements. Over her turtleneck she wore a long pink sweater he hadn't seen before. No wonder her luggage weighs so much. "I'm going to take your boots off. Tell me if it hurts." He carefully unlaced them and pulled the opening as wide as it would go on both boots.

"I did have them waterproofed…" Lisa said absently as she watched with rounded blue eyes, wincing when her toes exited the narrow opening.

"There," he said. "The worst is over. How are you doing?"

She smiled tentatively. "Toes tingle a bit." She reached down and pulled one set of damp wool socks off, exposing a thinner pair.

"Hang on. We need to get you into dry clothes first." He set the boots on the tile under the woodstove, trying to distract himself from the awkward task ahead. "After the boots dry, I'll waterproof them again." He touched her calf. "How're your legs?"

"My ankle? It feels okay. Must have been my immediate ice therapy." A smile softened her features. "Quick thinking, huh?"

"Must have been." He chuckled, happy to see she still had a sense of humor. Adam sat back on his foot. "Though, actually, your legs were the most exposed." He pressed on her calf again. "This hurt?"

She shook her head.

He wrapped his hand around her foot and squeezed gently. "This?"

"No, I don't feel a thing."

That wasn't a good sign, but he didn't want to worry her. "You have two choices. I can either carry you upstairs to change, or I can go get your dry clothes for you. Which would you prefer?"

The anxious look on her face told him she, too, felt the same awkwardness over the situation. What he wouldn't do to have his mother here right now, even though he was relieved to know she was safe.

Lisa's voice sounded raspy. "It's silly to be so modest over a few undergarments, isn't it? After all, they're just clothes."

Adam felt his heartbeat quicken and the corner of his mouth turn up despite his attempt to stop it. "I can't deny that, though it isn't quite the same in person. I didn't want to invade your privacy or I'd have grabbed you a fresh change." His smirk grew to a full-fledged smile. "Would it help if I promised not to peek?"

Color returned to her cheeks. "No," she said demurely. "If you'll help me up the stairs, I'm sure I can change on my own."

"You shouldn't put any weight on your feet. If there's frostbite, it could damage the skin tissue."

She swung her legs over the edge of the sofa and set them on the rug. The pain was immediately evident.

"Hang on, here we go." Adam wrapped a blanket around her and lifted her into the cradle of his arms. She locked her hands behind his neck.

"It's getting dark."

"Electricity is out." He felt the shiver spread through her body and he pulled her closer. "Don't worry, we'll be fine. It'll be warmer in my quarters. None of these fancy high ceilings. My grandparents didn't even have central heating until the fifties."

"You're kidding."

He felt the warmth of her breath on his face. "Nope, and they stayed plenty warm with the stoves. Of course, they didn't leave the ranch all winter."

He was glad he'd thought to install rechargeable emergency lights for the main hall and guest rooms. They not only lit the way but also provided enough light so Lisa could get what she needed.

Adam struggled to ignore the feelings he was having for the woman in his arms. She was an independent woman with her mind on the future and making a place for herself in the world. His own corner of it didn't fit into the jet-setter's scheme. He was nothing more than her current assignment. She needed him now, but that wouldn't last.

"I should probably use the rest room while I'm here. If you wouldn't mind, I'll change in there."

"Oh, okay. Make it quick. I don't want you away from the fire too long. While you change, I'll check the pipes in the other suites. If you need any help…I'll um…be right back." He set her down and handed her a towel to dry off, feeling like a sixteen-year-old and probably sounding even younger.

The smile on her face reassured him that she not only shared his discomfort, but also understood the meaning behind his words, despite his stumbling over each one. "Thanks, Adam. I'll call when I'm ready."

He carried her down the stairs a few minutes later. Lisa admired Adam's profile as he stoked the fire. He brushed a wisp of hair from his forehead and she wondered if it was the only unmanageable aspect of his life.

Lisa lowered her hand over the edge of the sofa and ran her fingers over Toby's soft black fur. Toby had followed them into Adam's house, planting himself protectively by her side.

Adam pushed himself to his full height and glanced over his shoulder. The outline of his athletic physique stretched the waffle-weave fabric of his shirt. He pushed up the sleeves, exposing his muscular forearms. "You warming up?"

Lisa tried to shut out the images of Adam's strong arms holding her, catching her, embracing her. "I'm feeling much better. Thanks."

"Time to check your feet." Adam pulled a cast-iron teakettle from the woodstove and poured water into a plastic basin. "Just a sec." A few moments later he arrived with an ice-cream bucket of snow.

Lisa pulled the blanket tighter around her. "You know, there's plenty of the white stuff outside and I really don't care to save any for nostalgia's sake."

Adam smiled, softening the worry lines on his face. "I need to cool this water down." He scooped snow into the steaming water. He knelt before her, lifted the blanket off her legs and gently pulled the sock from her foot.

Toby whimpered, and Lisa patted his head. "It's okay, boy." She leaned forward to look at her feet. They were unusually white. "How bad is it?"

Adam pulled the sock from her other foot. She ran her fingers over the puffy ankle.

"Don't rub. You have a mild case of frostbite." He gently surrounded her toes with his hands. "Don't get too close to the fire...you won't be able to tell if they get too warm." He pulled the basin to the edge of the sofa and added a little more water.

He turned his hand palm up and dripped water onto it. "Cooled it off too much." He added another glug of hot water, repeating the procedure until he seemed pleased with the temperature.

"Looks like you've fed your share of babies."

He laughed. "Only calves. My sisters and Emily breast-fed. And when they had to give them bottles, it took a more experienced hand than Uncle Adam's."

She watched his callused hands lift each foot into the water with amazing tenderness. Adam squeezed liquid over her feet and lower legs with a washcloth, then with a baby-soft touch, he massaged. "Wiggle your toes while I get us a warm drink."

"You don't have to wait on me." She moved.

He rested a hand on her shoulder. "Actually, I do, and I will. For the next few hours at least, I'm your servant, so what'll you have—homemade cherry cider, cocoa or coffee?"

"Homemade cider?"

"A lady from the local church has an orchard in the Devil's Backbone area. She makes cider, jelly and pies. We live for cherry season. Which sounds good?"

Her body slumped back against the cushions. "I think I'd like to try the cider. Thanks." Lisa heard Adam pull things from the cupboard. Soon after, he set a pan on the wood-burning stove, then filled it with the red liquid. The tart aroma filled the room like a garden in blossom.

"Any feeling in your feet yet?"

"Unfortunately, yes. The pain just started."

He set another towel on the carpet. Adam took Lisa's feet from the water and carefully blotted them dry. "That means the blood is circulating again."

She uncovered her feet and examined them. "They're all red. The water didn't seem that hot."

"It wasn't. That's normal, too." He poured her a mug of cider and handed it to her. She wrapped her hands around the mug and felt the warmth seep through her body, startled to realize she was still chilled. "Put your feet up and relax. I'll get you some roomy socks, then I'll see what I can find for supper."

Lisa sipped the cider and snuggled down into the sofa while she waited for his return.

She could hear his sturdy footsteps on the floor above. In a matter of minutes he was stretching soft thick socks over her feet, stuffing feather pillows behind under her back and tucking the soft fleece blanket around her. And then he was gone again.

While Adam called the lodge "home," she could see this was where he lived. It was still meticulously neat, but it was truer to the man himself. His ties to family were evident here. Pictures were everywhere. She stretched to reach the five-by-seven of Adam's mother and father. His dad was a handsome man who'd passed on a strong resemblance to his youngest son.

Bookshelves lined with novels included big-name authors, religious leaders and bestselling Western writers alike. Several versions of the Bible were stacked on the buffet next to the dining room window.

She looked into the blackness and wondered how much longer she could have survived the elements. One wiggle of her toes served to remind her how fortunate she'd been that Adam and Toby had come when they did.

"It was then that I carried you." Lisa closed her eyes. How could God...? She shoved the thought away. God didn't care about her. Not anymore. She hadn't been obedient so He had turned away just like her own father had two decades ago.

Adam entered the room, dropped a load of wood into the bin and added wood to the fire. "How does leftover soup sound?" The cast-iron door closed with a bang. "Lisa, are you okay? Do you need a painkiller?"

She opened her eyes, only then feeling the moisture trickle down her cheeks. "No, it's not bad."

He paused. "Oh. Sorry if I interrupted..."

She shrugged and wiped the tears away. More replaced them, and Lisa fought for control. She wasn't the crying type, but the more she tried to stop, the more emotion engulfed her body.

Adam disappeared and returned with a box of tissues. "If you'd like to talk..."

"No."

"Can I get you anything?"

"No," she snapped, avoiding his probing gaze.

Adam brushed the hair from her face, his rough

hands cooled her warm skin. "It's okay to cry, Lisa. It's even okay to let yourself need someone."

How tempting it would be to believe him, but that would only end in pain, as well. "Maybe in your world that works…"

"God's everywhere you are, Lisa. He's always there to comfort you and see you through rough times. He always has time to listen.…"

Her tears started all over again. How did Adam know what she was feeling and thinking? Lisa cleared her throat and shook her head. "Not to me."

Adam helped her sit up and make room for him. He pulled her back to his chest, wrapping his arms around her. "Imagine this is what God's arms feel like around you. You can't see Him, but He's there." Adam brushed her hair off her face. "He can feel your pain. He knows your invisible scars. He loves you anyway."

Lisa closed her eyes and drank in the comfort of Adam's nearness, tried to let his words erase doubt from her mind. She thought of the afternoon and gulped back a sob. "I was so afraid you wouldn't find me."

She felt his chest rise and fall in quick succession. "I was, too, until Toby showed up and led me across the valley." His breath was warm against her skin. "You see, God *is* your refuge. He took care of you until I could find you."

She struggled with conflicting emotions. "I never felt God was real. I heard the words, but never really *felt* Him.'' Lisa didn't mean to tell Adam that, but now that the words were out, it felt right. He would understand.

Adam leaned his face close to hers, his rough chin grazing her cheekbone. ''Now you can understand why I opened Whispering Pines Guest Ranch. I want guests to have a refuge from life, where they can feel God's presence, just like I did when my own life spun out of control.''

''You think my life is spinning out of control?''

He shook his head. ''Only you know why God brought you here, Lisa. But when you figure it out, would you let me know?''

She felt a certain sadness at his reply. Despite her attempts to shut out her feelings for Adam, each day they spent together, her feelings for him grew.

She couldn't forget the passion of that first kiss, or the tenderness of his arms, or the hope she felt just being around Adam MacIntyre.

Adam pushed her away and stood, adjusting the pillows again. ''Dinner will be ready in a minute.''

And then she was alone.

Lisa closed her eyes. *Why did You bring me here, God? How could You tempt me with a life I can never have?*

Chapter Sixteen

Candlelight, an attractive woman and a feeling of protectiveness were a lethal combination. After the turn their conversation had taken, Lisa probably needed a few minutes alone. He needed it even more.

Adam reminded himself that Lisa's days at the ranch were numbered. She needed a job. Wanted the career she'd trained for. He couldn't blame her for that. Not every woman considered life on a secluded ranch a career goal.

He looked around. There would be a lifetime of work here, that much was sure, but he'd learned quickly that being self-employed meant there was no guarantee of that monthly paycheck or benefits package. He couldn't ask her to give up her dreams for a ranch that was more in the red than ever before.

He had to keep his distance. When the lights came

back on, he didn't want either of them to have any regrets. Lisa had had enough broken promises.

He poured the jar of leftover vegetable beef soup into a pot and set it on the gas stove to heat while he stepped outside with Toby. Adam took a deep breath of the cold air. *Lord, I can't see beyond my own desires right now. I've fallen in love with Lisa, and I'm not at all sure that's the best thing. It's happened so fast. She's hurting so much, and I'm not at all sure how to help her. Show me Your plan, Father. And if it's not meant to be, give me the strength to let her go.*

"Toby, come." The dog greeted Adam with a cheerful bark, seemingly energized by the cold air. Adam brushed the snow from his long fur and opened the door. Toby made a beeline directly to Lisa.

Adam dished up two mugs of soup and tucked a package of crackers under his chin. At least the meal was hot and nourishing. Gourmet didn't matter much at the moment. Lisa had to be exhausted. Once she ate, she'd probably fall asleep.

When he entered the living room, she pulled her knees toward her body, making room for him on the sofa. *So much for keeping my distance.* He handed her a mug and moved for the chair next to the sofa, hoping she wouldn't argue. "You were comfortable. Go ahead and stretch out. It's easier to visit this way."

"It smells wonderful." She reached for the crack-

ers, the light of his grandmother's oil lamp illumi-
nating her golden hair and warm smile.

"There's plenty, so eat up." Adam tore his gaze
from Lisa and blew into his soup.

Lisa gave him an odd look as she tested the temperature of hers. "You're a terrific host. Where did
you learn to take such good care of everyone?"

His ego needed a boost, but not from a woman
who would be gone in a matter of days. He fought
the longing to try to change her mind. "Being the
youngest, I was the family gofer."

Lisa crinkled her nose. "A gopher?"

"Yeah, as in, 'Adam, run get this... Bring me that
medicine...'" His voice faded out. "You know, go
for—gofer. Surely your mom and sisters..."

She shook her head and looked at him with
amused wonder. "Our childhoods were so different." Her voice was still soft and husky from the
cold weather. "How old were you when your dad
got sick?"

His jaw tightened. "Fifteen." It wasn't exactly
light conversation, but it would keep his mind off
Lisa. Adam stretched his legs in front of him and
cradled the soup mug in the palm of one hand. He
went on to tell her stories about their many trips to
the ice cream shop and secret fishing excursions.

Lisa envied Adam. Even in their worst times, he
had wonderful memories. His childhood had been
worlds apart from hers. They had pets and family
vacations, silly pictures and family reunions that con-

tinued to draw them together. Emily and Kat had tried in recent years to create that kind of bond, but they had lost years that could never be replaced.

Lisa felt tears sting her eyes and blinked them away. "Tell me more about your dad."

Adam finished chewing a cracker and pushed his chin forward. He paused for a drink, then shrugged. "You don't want to hear—"

"Yes, I do." Surprised, Lisa nodded, realizing for the first time that she longed to know his dad, even if only vicariously.

Confusion clouded his eyes. "Why?"

Did talking about his dad dig up painful emotions Adam didn't want to face? "I'm curious..." *Nosy* felt more like it. Lisa felt her cheeks warm. "Never mind. I didn't mean to pry."

"It's not that. Suddenly I feel...guilty."

"Why would you feel guilty?"

"Because I had a dad, and you didn't. Because I have great memories, and you don't. Because I don't want to make the emptiness you must feel even worse."

How could she argue with that? She took a deep breath and let it out, willing the tears away. "You couldn't make it any worse, Adam. I know billions of people had wonderful fathers, and from the men you and your brothers are now, yours had to have been one of the best. You look like him." She smiled, noting the question on Adam's face. "He was very handsome."

One corner of his mouth turned up. "Indirect compliments work for me."

"I hope so. Were you like him in personality?"

Adam shrugged. "Yeah, I guess. I never really thought that much about it."

"So he was tough on the outside and a softy inside?" From his silence, Lisa guessed Adam didn't much appreciate her assessment. She glanced up, daring to smile.

He studied her thoughtfully for a moment, holding her gaze tenderly in his. "No comment."

Pleased that she had successfully disarmed him with her smile, she repeated her request. "Tell me more about him."

Adam granted her wish. "One Saturday morning Dad insisted he had to give me a driving lesson." He chuckled. "Mom argued that I had chores and homework, but she finally gave in. It wasn't like either of them to argue." Adam glanced at the photo on the end table. "I'd never driven anywhere besides the school parking lot or here at the ranch in the pasture. We had an old beat-up truck that I was allowed to use, but this day, Dad insisted we take his new Jeep to the mountains."

Lisa finished eating then rested her head on the pillows, listening to Adam's touching account of the afternoon four-wheeling and fishing with his father.

"We took every back road in the county, finding every fishing hole around. There I was, barely able to drive on a city street, yet Dad had to teach me the ins and outs of mountain driving, including roads that weren't roads at all. I was petrified.''

Much as Lisa tried to imagine Adam fifteen and scared, she couldn't. "But you passed with flying colors, right?"

He shook his head. "Not exactly. Dad told me to cross this stream..." Adam's mouth curved to an unconscious smile. "Only, it was a lot deeper than he thought and we washed downstream...."

She raised to one elbow. "What happened?"

"Oh, we didn't go far—a boulder stopped us. I thought I was dead. His Jeep was brand-new."

"What did he do—ground you?"

"His eyes were huge. I was sure he'd blow his top, but he laughed. He opened the door, looked at the water rushing by and said, 'That's a lot deeper than it was last week.' Then he launched into a lesson on using the wench, which we proceeded to do to get ourselves out.'' Adam slipped into a trance. "Dad always found a way to make lemonade out of lemons. We had some fun times before he got too sick. If Mom had known, *she'd* have grounded us both for life.''

"I'm sure your mom would be thrilled to know how special those times ended up being to you. You ought to tell her. She'd probably laugh now.'' Millie impressed her as the type of woman who didn't hold on to the past, but looked forward to tomorrow.

She felt uncomfortable under Adam's gentle and contemplative gaze and looked away.

"What memories do you have of your dad?" Adam's question startled her.

Silence filled the emptiness and he waited patiently. "I don't. I used to make up stories about him to try to convince myself that I remembered him. A few years ago, Katarina asked me to help her find him." Lisa remembered the hurt in her sister's voice when she refused. "I couldn't."

"Aren't you at all curious about him?"

"Curious enough that every town I travel to I look up his name in the phone book, but not brave enough to make the call if I ever did find him. One rejection is enough to survive. Twice..." She realized she'd almost opened up the topic of Dale again. "He doesn't want to know me. I don't need him."

Lisa avoided looking at Adam. She couldn't withstand his silent appraisal right now. "So you don't let yourself need anyone? You won't let anyone need you? You keep moving so that you don't have to make too big of a commitment."

"It's called survival. I do what I have to do."

"You're missing out on life, Lisa. You need to let someone take care of you, let them need you, love you..."

Her heart raced. She wanted to leave. "They'll only leave again. They always do. People make promises and then they break them. They take what they want...and then they go."

"We're not talking about your dad anymore, are

we?'' Adam's voice was quiet, but his tone demanded the truth.

"Why are you doing this to me? Because you think I can't leave?'' She threw the covers from her lap and set her feet on the floor. "Hands and knees are good enough for Alissa. They'll work for me.''

Adam knelt next to her. "I'm doing this because I care about you. But as long as this pain consumes you..." He rubbed his hand over his forehead. "Don't you see what you're missing?''

She pulled his hand away from his face and looked him in the eyes. "Don't you think I've tried? I finally let myself need someone, and he literally took my life away. He took everything—my furniture, my clothes, my photography equipment..." Adam's forehead creased with the twitch of his brow.

"The boyfriend?''

She nodded.

Adam sat on the edge of the sofa. "Go on.''

"We were a team—he took the pictures, I wrote the stories. I wanted to learn everything he knew about photography.'' She looked down at her hands, and Adam lifted her chin. "I turned down a job to move across the country and work with him. When I came to Katarina and Alex's wedding, he had an important assignment and needed to borrow my brand-new digital camera. It was my graduation gift from my family. When I got home, the apartment was empty. I couldn't even pay rent. I had to replace my equipment.''

"You never found him?"

She shrugged. "Why would I even bother looking for a jerk like him? He'd moved out the day after I flew to Colorado, Adam. He hocked my personal things, kept my equipment and left."

Adam's lips parted in amazement. "You're a fighter, Lisa. Why didn't you go after him? Why didn't you press charges?"

"With no money?" Lisa shook her head. "Sometimes the best way to win a battle is not to get into the fight in the first place. He'd already taken all my material belongings and broken my heart. I couldn't afford to lose anything more."

"You had no clue he'd do something like that?"

She shifted her gaze away from the concern of his gentle brown eyes. "I knew Dale had some expensive habits, but I thought he'd given them up— I was naive. No, I didn't ever believe he'd hurt me."

Adam took hold of her hand. "You didn't tell your sisters, did you? They would have helped. That's what family is for, Lisa."

"They had their own lives, new husbands, jobs, orphaned little boys, babies... They didn't need to worry about their gullible baby sister. Besides, survival keeps the mind pretty busy. Helping out in the shelters, I realized very quickly, I could have been a lot worse off."

Adam's eyes softened. "Yes, I guess it could have been worse."

She heard her heart beat faster the longer Adam

remained quiet. His silence aroused old fears and uncertainties. Did he think she was a coward? Was it because she'd admitted to living with someone?

Lisa buried her face in the pillows. Better she find out now if Adam couldn't forgive her past, before she'd given her heart to him. And if his interest was genuine, better he know from the start that a relationship with her would be an uphill battle. Try as she may, her insecurities weren't easy to overcome.

"I'll be right back."

Lisa looked at her watch, surprised to see it was nearly ten. With the day she'd had, she should be asleep by now. She closed her eyes, not expecting Adam to return anytime soon.

A soft melody drifted into the room. Adam set the battery-operated compact disk player on the kitchen counter. "I think this dance is long overdue."

She looked around. "But…"

Adam knelt down and lifted her into his arms, and she locked her hands behind his neck. He cradled her close as he did his best to dance around the furniture without hitting her feet against anything. "I'm not much of a dancer, but I think I can safely promise not to step on your toes."

She smiled. "You know how I feel about promises."

"I aim to change your mind about that, if you'll give me the chance."

When she tried to speak, her voice wavered. "It

doesn't bother you that I lived with someone?'' She leaned away to watch his expression, and waited.

His eyes didn't leave hers for an instant. ''If you or I were the first to make that mistake, there would be no hope. Jesus died for all of our sins.''

She studied his face unhurriedly, feature by feature. ''I wanted to be sure, now, before things get any more complicated.''

''That's the most optimism I've heard out of you yet.'' One corner of his mouth turned up. ''You really think there's a chance things between us could get complicated?''

She felt the promise in his gaze, in his smile, in his soft laughter. ''With your brothers married to my sisters, I'd say it already is complicated.''

''Leave them out of it.''

She brushed the stray hair from his forehead. ''My life is on the road, yours is firmly grounded to responsibilities here. I'd still say it's already complicated.'' She leaned her head on his shoulder and Adam sat down. He held her close and neither of them spoke for a long while.

''Please don't make matters worse by not facing reality, Adam. I am who I am, and you have to know from the start—''

Adam cleared his throat. ''Let's take it one day at a time. Right now, you're here, so let's make the most of getting to know one another before you leave.''

Chapter Seventeen

She and Adam talked late into the night in the dim glow of the lantern. When Adam woke just after two in the morning with Lisa in his embrace, the fire had died out and the windows already frosted over. He eased Lisa aside, rested her head on the pillow and tucked the blankets around her. *Father, help me resist temptation.* He brushed the silky hair off of her face and she rolled over, mumbling softly. The waffled texture of his shirt had left an imprint on her cheek.

He started fires in both his private quarters and the lodge. It wouldn't take long for them to warm up again. Though he knew she'd be okay, he couldn't leave her downstairs by herself. Adam pulled the comforter from his bed and returned to the chair next to Lisa and went back to sleep.

Woken by the faint sound of the rooster crowing,

Adam moved quietly about the house. He added another log to the fire, then proceeded through the lodge, checking for frozen pipes. Everything looked fine. He paused in the doorway of the deluxe suite, pleased with the progress in the past week. He couldn't have done it without Lisa. The thought frightened him. Terrified him. Made him come face-to-face with the realization that the lodge wasn't the only thing that had changed since Lisa's arrival.

He didn't want to need anyone, especially not an independent woman who lived life with her foot on the accelerator. He'd set aside that lifestyle long ago.

When Adam went downstairs, Lisa stood at the door, watching Toby run through the drifts, some of which were as tall as the giant of a dog. "It must have snowed all night," she said.

Adam joined her, but she just stared outside with her back to him.

"You're okay, Lisa."

"Must have been my guardian angel."

He rested his hand on her shoulder. "God appointed one especially to you."

"Are you implying that I need extra attention?" Her eyebrow quirked upward and a smile teased her lips.

He'd resisted kissing Lisa last night, but it was going to take another long talk with God this morning to refrain much longer. "Don't take it too personally. He appoints at least one to each of His children." Adam turned to watch the black puppy jump and play. "I haven't seen this much snow here since I was in grade school. We had to bend down to see in the windows."

She turned her head and studied him for a long moment. "And you think I'm one of God's children?"

Adam wrapped his arms around her. "I know you are. He loves you Lisa and He's ready for you to hand your life to Him."

Silence.

She reached over and flipped the light switch. "Nothing yet." Lisa stared out the window in a trance. She crossed her arms over her body.

Adam stood behind her and rubbed her upper arms "You cold?"

She shook her head. "No, just a sudden chill. How long until they have the power back on?"

"It could be days. The radio says the whole area is without power. Town will be the first priority. Those of us out here are expected to be prepared for such emergencies. Part of the joys of rural life, doesn't matter the season. Thunderstorms or snow— all affects us about the same." She wanted reality, and unfortunately, it was coming in handfuls this week. If this storm didn't let up soon, it would scare her away before he stood a chance of tempting her to stay. "How about a board game marathon after breakfast? We used to do that when the school called a snow day. Makes time go pretty fast."

Her eyes didn't leave the snow. "What games do you have?"

"Every game ever made for the past forty years." He stepped up beside her and turned her away from the window. "Let's have some oatmeal by the fire."

She turned back around. "Where's Toby?"

"Probably checking on the cattle. He'll be fine. He led me to you, remember?"

"Oh, yeah. He's a rescue dog, right?"

"He's actually best in the water. We have a lot of reservoirs in the area. Summer seems to bring out all the partyers." Toby appeared at the back door and shook the snow from his fur. Lisa let him in, obviously relieved to see her protector. She took the towel from the coat hook and dried him off. "So how did you decide to become a search-and-rescue team?"

"It kind of started out as a joke. Alex thought Toby would be a perfect companion since I've always sworn I'd never get married. He and Kevin went to the rescue shelter and came to work one day with Toby."

"Kind of an expensive joke, isn't it?"

He chuckled. "They would have never committed me to caring for a dog without knowing I'd love one. My golden retriever died last winter. Until they brought Toby home, I was dead set against ever having another pet. You know brothers. They insisted I'd be less crabby if I had company. If yesterday is any indication of his tracking ability, we're going to make a good team.''

Adam was surprised to see Lisa's mood improve as the day went on. She stayed inside while he tended to chores. After he'd finished with those, they worked rearranging the suites, hanging pictures and adding the little details such as cabinet handles and outlet covers.

After two days, the sun finally came out, and on the third day, electricity was restored. Everything had technically gone fine, but Adam had worried that Lisa would go stir-crazy without her laptop and cell phone, which had gone dead by the end of the first day. Not surprisingly, she had found countless ways to fill her time.

As soon as the snow had stopped, Adam attached a blade to the front of an old truck and began the tedious job of plowing the entrance to the ranch. He'd just finished plowing his mother's drive when Kevin, Emily and Millie arrived with the children.

Lisa ran out the door to greet their guests, obviously relieved to have contact with the outside world again. ''We've been trying to call for days,'' Emily said, then exchanged hugs with her sister.

''The land lines are still out as far as I know, but a visit is better than a phone call anyday, isn't it, Alissa?'' Lisa snuggled their adorable curly-haired niece and Adam found himself imagining what their kids would look like. Did she even want children?

Adam lagged behind with Kevin, forcing his mind from his futile love life. He laughed at Toby and Ricky playing in the snow. "This reminds me of that spring break when they had four feet of snow here."

Kevin nodded. "Yeah, the sledding was great."

"Until Mom sent you to your room for hooking Tike up to pull the sled." Adam laughed while recalling their sheltie wondering what happened.

Kevin nudged him. "Keep your voice down. We don't want to give Ricky any ideas."

"Something tells me your son will have enough all on his own without borrowing ideas, bro."

Adam felt his mother's eyes on him the minute he and Kevin walked in the door. She followed his every move from hanging his coat on the hook to leaving his boots on the rug. He realized exactly why the minute his gaze landed on Lisa.

His mom's face brightened with her usual "I knew it all along" expression. "Looks like you both came through the storm fine."

Adam nodded, wishing she wasn't so observant. "We managed just fine. A blizzard, Lisa can handle, no contact with the outside world on the other hand—"

"I managed," Lisa interrupted, "I have eight phone messages to return, I'll have you know."

"Why am I not surprised?" he said before thinking. He realized they were bantering as easily as any married couple. Noting the grin on her sister's face, he wasn't the only one to pick up on it, either.

He was hanging himself with his own rope. "Lisa, why don't you have Emily take a look at your ankle? Have you told her what happened?"

"No, I haven't had a chance. She didn't have her cell phone on, but I did reach Katarina." She helped hang everyone's coats, then added, "Let's go to the living room."

Emily's expression turned to concern as she took the lead to the lodge. "What happened?"

Lisa took a step toward Adam's private living room before realizing the others were going to the lodge. Adam winked, silently acknowledging her mistake. Everyone listened intently while she and Adam told about the blizzard, each filling in on what the other missed.

"There was one good thing that came as a result of the storm," Adam added. "Your sister finally realized God's keeping track of her after all. Of course, first He had to find a way to get her to slow down so He could get her to listen…"

Lisa blushed. "So I'm a little more difficult to catch up with. Haven't you ever heard the saying 'Never drive faster than your angels can fly'? Well, I can now verify, that applies to planes, trains, taxis and snowshoes."

"God must have assigned you an angel for each time zone." Adam's retort was so quick, it sounded like they'd been through this discussion before.

"Before you change the subject, I want Emily to make sure everything is healing okay. You were sitting in that snow quite a while." Lisa hoped she was the only one to notice the tenderness in Adam's voice.

Why did she feel as if she was suddenly the center of attention? Had she missed something?

Kevin interrupted the silence. "Why don't you two go on upstairs? Adam and I can unload Mom's van."

Millie immediately accepted the offer, defending her shopping trip for emergency rations while the boys teased her about how quickly the snow would be melted.

Emily paused to look out the front window. "Looks like Ricky thinks you need a lot of angels, Lisa."

The five-year-old jumped up from the snowdrift, moved a couple feet over and flopped into the snow. He spread his arms and legs, then jumped up again.

"Well, it never hurts to have a few extra around." She knelt down and picked up her niece and led the way up the stairs to her suite. "I'm feeling much better. This really isn't necessary."

"I think it was the guys' way of giving us a little time to talk privately." Emily followed her into Lisa's suite and closed the door.

"And what might we need to talk about?"

"Let's see... The youngest MacIntyre brother and the youngest Berthoff sister are stranded and alone for three days—speculation is there could be a lot to talk about.'' Emily smiled, ready to broadcast the news with the slightest hint of confirmation.

Lisa miraculously managed to suppress a smile. "So Millie's stay to help Kat *was* a ruse, huh?"

Emily laughed. "Not exactly. Katarina did need help with the bookkeeping and Millie is a tremendous help. And the birthday party went great, thanks to her help. But that's not why we're here."

Lisa sat on the bed and took her slippers and socks off. "So…these are my toes. They hurt quite a bit at first, still tingle if I bang them on something."

"So do mine." Her sister gave Lisa a critical squint before she began examining them. "Somehow, I suspect it wasn't your toes Adam wanted me to examine. Frostbite on the hands and feet is pretty basic, even for an E.M.T."

"A what?" Lisa felt her face flush.

"Emergency Medical Technician. It's part of the search-and-rescue training. Didn't he tell you?" Emily laughed. "Practical application is the most difficult for beginners, especially when the victim is a personal friend. Adam probably figured I'd be out here soon enough. Come on, sis, let's finish the exam." Emily asked question after question before giving Lisa a clean bill of health. "I'll make sure to have a follow-up consultation with the E.M.T. Make sure he has no other concerns about your case."

Lisa bit her tongue. "If you're fishing for a story, you've come to the wrong place."

Emily opened Alissa's bag and pulled out a disposable diaper. "I don't know. This is a romantic getaway." She lifted the baby to the bed and quickly changed her. "Not only that, Tara called Kevin to get the scoop on you. She became quite concerned when she couldn't reach Adam that evening."

"She did? And what did Kevin tell her?"

Emily shrugged. "You know Kevin. He said he wasn't sure, but it was probably an old girlfriend."

Lisa burst out laughing. She missed times like this. She missed the closeness of family and friends. "Thanks for the laugh."

"And you're still not going to tell me anything?"

Lisa bit her lip. She truly hadn't expected this from either family. Adam's initial reaction to her arrival made more sense now. "Adam's been a wonderful host and a perfect gentleman. That's it."

"Maybe Kevin had better luck with Adam."

Lisa's cellular phone rang, and she welcomed the interruption. Emily took Alissa downstairs, allowing Lisa privacy to take the call.

When Lisa finished, she joined them in the middle of Adam's tour of the suites. Soon after, Millie said gave Lisa a warm hug and invited them to church.

"We'll be there," they all answered in unison.

Adam's look showed his surprise, but he didn't mention it. He gave his mother a warm hug. "I appreciate your help, Mom."

"I know you do, honey. This storm set everything behind schedule. Since you and Lisa have already taken care of the suites, I'll return these things Monday.'' Millie gave her granddaughter a big kiss and thanked Kevin and Emily for following her out to the ranch. Adam walked her to the van then turned back toward the house with Ricky slung over his shoulder.

Lisa tried to ignore the pitter-patter of her heart at Adam's tenderness for his mother. With each step he took, her heart raced a little faster. She felt Kevin and Emily watching her, and tried to ignore her own reaction. She watched as his long legs made short time of the distance between them.

Emily gave Lisa a hug. ''We need to get going. I'm glad you decided to come tomorrow.'' She looked at Lisa one more time as Adam reached for the doorknob. ''Do you really expect me to believe you can ignore a good-looking cowboy like Adam?''

''Better luck next time, sis.''

Chapter Eighteen

Lisa's mind was still spinning. If she accepted the job, she had to leave. If she didn't, who knew when an opportunity like this would come again?

Nothing could ever be more wonderful than spending the last few days with Adam. He was right. God had revealed a lot to her here in the solitude of Whispering Pines. But now it was over.

She took a deep breath and gathered her courage when she heard the door close. His voice echoed from the beamed ceilings. "Your sister is suspicious."

With good reason. Why was it she and Adam were the only ones caught off balance by their feelings for one another? Falling in love was the furthest thing from her mind when she'd stepped onto that jet in San Francisco two weeks ago.

Francie accused Lisa of letting her personal feelings interfere with this assignment. She couldn't argue with that, even though she had never been the type to use sensationalism in order to sell a story. After all, what was more romantic than a man who honored his family and wanted to share his heritage with others? She didn't need to embellish the facts.

She wouldn't back down. She'd send Francie her article. If she and Steve didn't like it, that was their problem, not hers. If she didn't get the full-time job with their magazine, something would come up elsewhere. Today's phone call proved that.

Where God closes a door, He always opens a window. How often had she heard Emily say those words?

"Lisa? Is everything okay?"

She stared blankly at Adam. "Great. I— I may have another assignment."

She watched reality sink in. They had both been so intent on their budding relationship that they'd overlooked how quickly things could change. Even she had set reality aside. Though the past few weeks were unforgettable, it was long past time for her to get moving again. Lisa realized that now.

Adam leaned against the stair railing and pulled her into his embrace. "Is it an assignment for the magazine, or an interview for someone else?"

"I'll be doing a shoot for an exclusive catalog."

"No story?" His brown eyes searched hers and Lisa felt as if she had somehow deceived him.

"I can be silenced, for the right price." She managed a tentative smile. "This is a golden opportunity and the income is extraordinary. They need someone with outdoor photography experience."

He looked at her through narrowed eyes and shook his head. "But you're a photojournalist. I assumed…"

"I'm a freelancer—I do whatever brings an income, and right now, a woman in this business can't overlook having a backup plan. The photographer was fired and there's a possibility it could turn into a regular assignment."

Adam forced a smile. "That's great."

"Funny thing is, I have the oddest feeling the photographer was my ex-boyfriend." The words were out before she even realized what she was saying.

Icy contempt flashed in his eyes and his body tensed. "What makes you think that?"

She relished the time spent in Adam's protective embrace, even if doing so would make it that much more difficult to leave. "The editor got my name from a model that I met when I was in Portland. The only job I've ever done there was with Dale."

"I don't like the sound of this."

"He can't hurt me." She took a deep breath. "Whatever this photographer did landed him in jail."

"Jail? Lisa…"

"I'll be fine, Adam. If it is Dale, he's already behind bars."

"If it's him, you could press charges."

"Press charges? No. I—I couldn't."

"Why not? He ruined your life."

"No. Dale may have changed it, but leaving was the best thing that he ever did for me." Lisa felt trapped between her words and the truth. She'd read those self-help articles on finding happiness and letting go of the past—even written a few. While she could say the words and put on a brave front, inside her heart still raced like a coward's. "He's the *last* person I plan to see. Forget I mentioned him, okay?" She kissed Adam. "Please."

He nodded unconvincingly. "What about the party? And pictures? I thought you'd stay to help."

She felt a warm sensation pass between them. "I'll be here. I told the editor I have to be back here by Saturday. She said she'd check the budget." Lisa faltered. If they wouldn't pay for her return ticket, she'd do so. "Don't worry, I'll be here. In the meantime, I need to pick up my camera and try it out. What do you say we go take some pictures?"

He looked around. "But the lodge isn't ready."

"It looks fine."

"Fine leaves room for improvement. We're talking national exposure here. I've tried to make it homey, but it's still missed something. What is it?"

Homey? How would she know? She hadn't lived anywhere long enough to know what a home was supposed to feel like, but she had to admit—Whispering Pines Guest Ranch would be at the top of her list.

"It doesn't need much, really. You might put some of the family pictures from your living room out here on the table, fabric over the windows or maybe some tab curtains at some point. Candles, or crafty things, pillows…which reminds me…" She spun from his embrace and ran up the stairs. "Close your eyes. You can't peek."

She pulled the moose and the beaver from the bag and held them close. They were soft and cuddly, a perfect reminder of Adam.

"Are your eyes closed?" Lisa called as she walked out of her room and down the stairs.

He turned to face her, eyes closed. "Tight as the barn door."

She held both the stuffed animals behind her back, just in case he peeked. Lisa walked right up to Adam and lifted her chin. "Okay, you can open."

"I think it's rude to kiss with open eyes, don't you?" He didn't wait for an answer. Adam reached up and touched her face, exploring as if he were blind. His lips finally met hers, the kiss so tender it brought tears to her eyes. Keep it simple, Lisa.

When she thought Adam was ending the kiss, it lingered on. He held her with one hand on each shoulder, as if he sensed her weakening knees. She savored every moment.

"Wow. What store sells kisses like that?" He opened his eyes and stole one more kiss.

She felt the blood rush to her face. She blinked,

trying to shake the dizziness. "You were holding out on me."

Was she imagining it, or was he blushing, too?

Adam grinned mischievously. "And what about you? I don't recall your arms leaving your side."

"They were sort of busy—" she pulled the stuffed animals from behind her back "—trying to hold on to these." Lisa held her breath. She hoped he liked them. "I couldn't resist. You wanted rustic, and I thought these looked pretty rugged, in a cuddly sort of way. Maybe they'll add that homey feel."

Adam held them up. "They're cute little critters. Thank you." He snuggled them to his face and smiled. "Now, I guess we should go into town for the camera. Since you'll be leaving soon, maybe we could make it a date. If you wouldn't mind an evening out."

"Mind?" Lisa smiled. "I'd love it. Let me go change into something more suitable."

Adam realized he hadn't even asked where Lisa would be going. Did he even have her cell phone number? He changed into tan slacks and a black turtleneck, pulled on his boots and rushed down the stairs to wait.

A few minutes later, she was ready. She looked beautiful. He liked the way Lisa had pulled her hair up with loose honey-colored tendrils softening her face. With a fuzzy red vest and black turtleneck, Lisa wore a short charcoal-colored skirt and black tights that made her legs look longer and shapelier than he had imagined.

She looked self-conscious. "Is this okay? I don't have many dress clothes. They don't travel well."

He cleared his throat. "Don't apologize. You look…fine."

She placed a hand on her hip and gave herself another critical assessment. "Fine? According to you, fine isn't much of a compliment."

Adam would have swallowed the lump in his throat if he'd had enough saliva left. "Trust me, you look mighty nice, and I think that's about as much as I should say on the subject."

With his approval, Lisa let out a deep breath and relaxed her shoulders. Her giggle was contagious. "I don't date much, but that sounds like a compliment to me. Will it be okay for church? It's my only dress."

"You can go in whatever you're comfortable wearing, though I might add those tights don't look very warm for a woman who's recovering from frostbite."

"The clogs are lined with wool. And the tights are very warm. I was wearing them under my heavy leggings that day. According to Emily, there's no skin damage, but thanks for watching out for me."

He opened his mouth to say it was just part of his job, but he knew that wasn't the truth. It was totally personal now, and he didn't dare admit that yet. He didn't argue. If he did, they'd never make it to the camera store in time.

"You could have mentioned at least once that you're a trained medic."

"I didn't tell you because I'm not certified yet." He helped her into the four-wheel-drive truck and backed out of the drive, determined to change Lisa's mind about leaving.

Once they reached the highway, the roads were dry. He hoped it either got hot enough this next week to dry the roads out completely or stayed cold all week so they'd stay frozen. Otherwise, it was going to be a messy Valentine's Day celebration. Colorado weather could be pretty fickle. He recalled recent years when they'd taken picnics to the canyon in February and spent Kevin's Fourth of July birthday in sweatshirts huddled by the campfire.

"Adam?"

He turned. "Sorry, I was thinking about the weather. What did you say?"

Lisa tugged at the hem of her skirt. Even seated, it came just above the knee. "I was saying that in order to survive as a freelancer, I have to be flexible. I can't afford to turn down jobs—any job. I hope you understand."

"You must be a very good photographer if they want you to work for a catalog."

She felt the heat rise to her cheeks. "I'm not the best, but I am good. And I'm not kidding myself. They called because they're desperate. I'm affordable, I'm reliable and I'm available. That's important in this business. They need you where and when they need you." The traffic in town was thick with weekend shoppers. "The catalog is behind schedule, which costs them big money. This is my break. There's no room for mistakes. Some aspiring apprentice is always waiting for a chance, too."

"And you're the apprentice waiting in the wings?"

"It's a great opportunity. Fashion photography, if you can break in, pays extremely well."

"That's not what I asked. Were you his apprentice?"

"Yes, that's how we met." The cab of the truck was silent except for the sound of traffic whizzing past. "Would you mind if I leave some things at the ranch? If this job goes like others, we'll work till we drop. I thought it might be nice to travel light for a change."

"I don't know that that's possible," Adam stated matter-of-factly. "You traveling light, I mean." He turned off of Main Street. "I saw what two days without e-mail did to you, I can't imagine you without your laptop for a week."

He exaggerated the words, unable to hide a smile, and Lisa was happy to see him teasing her instead of pulling away again. "The hotel will have a computer and I can check my e-mail on my cell phone."

"What will they think of next? Speaking of which,

I want your phone number and e-mail address.''
Adam parked and turned off the engine.

She pulled a business card from her pack and gave
it to him. "I'll be right back. Warm up your smile."

Adam leaned his head on the seat, fingering the
card. "God, give me the strength to let her go. And
grant us the love that will bring her back home
again."

Chapter Nineteen

Lisa pulled the door open and scooted to the middle of the seat with a camera in each hand. The owner of the store climbed in behind her. "Bob offered to take pictures of the two of us and he also wants to show me how to use the latest digital camera. He says there should be some cleared sidewalks at one of the nearby parks."

They'd only been outside ten minutes before the roll of film was shot and Bob began to show Lisa the new one, after which, they returned to the store. Adam watched as Bob downloaded the pictures onto the computer, giving Lisa his best sales pitch.

"It's great," Lisa agreed. "And I admit, I loved my digital for a lot of things, but then again, all the technology in the world can't replace my Nikon. I'll think about it and let you know. I'm really not sure it's the right time to get another camera and upgrade my laptop.''

She paid for the camera repair and left her cell phone number for Bob to call when he'd finished developing the roll of her and Adam. "So what did you think of modeling?" she asked as they left.

Adam shook his head. "It wasn't too bad, but I hope no one saw us. I'd never live it down. Let's put it this way. My price just went up.''

Lisa's eyebrows arched and her smile widened. "And what is it now?''

"Dinner, custody of all the pictures of you and half of those with us together.''

She let out a laugh. "You must have been a tough businessman in your previous career.'' She didn't mention to Adam that he could make a lot more than that as a model, or that she'd checked with Bob about the possibility of doing some local work. He'd agreed to pass her name around and let her know if he heard of any job possibilities. She'd learned long ago to leave a string of strong bridges everywhere she went.

Adam nodded. "I was, but that was a long time ago. Any other errands you need to take care of?''

"I thought I'd look for new snow boots, so a sporting goods store, and then a discount store where I can replenish a few necessities.'' She took out her list and checked off the brick of film, spare batteries and a polarizer.

Her cell phone rang twice while Lisa was in the

dressing room; once Bob called to tell her the pictures had come out fine, the other was the catalog editor calling to agree to the terms Lisa had requested and give her the flight information.

Lisa shopped with her new assignment in mind since she would be spending a lot of time outside. She found thick socks, boots and a new pantsuit that would be well suited for traveling. She picked out silk pant liners to help hold in the warmth. After buying essentials at the discount store, Lisa begged Adam to stop at the mall to help her pick out another dress. "I'll be here next week, too, and I can't wear the same dress to church two weeks in a row."

"You wouldn't hear me complain." The magnetism of Adam's smile sent a twinge of guilt through her. She didn't want to dampen their last day together with thoughts of her leaving.

The afternoon went quickly, and before she knew it, they were on the highway. Adam picked a small, out-of-the-way restaurant with European cuisine. He chose the beef medallions in burgundy sauce and she ordered the rainbow trout.

When they arrived home, Adam pulled out a small package from all the bags they'd carried inside and invited her to sit in front of the fire.

She stared at the gift. "Where? How?"

"While you were trying dresses on, I slipped into another store. I knew just what I wanted. I hope you like it."

She looked at his square jaw, softened by a small

dimple she'd never noticed before. Lisa wasn't so sure how she should feel about the emotions invading her heart. The box was small, solid and heavy. And from the serious look on his face, it was a lot more than a moose or a beaver. She untied the ribbon and let it fall to her lap. Moments later, she was looking at a travel-size version of the Holy Bible.

"Adam, it's wonderful." She leaned into his embrace and lifted her lips to his. "A couple of whimsical stuffed animals don't quite compare."

He kissed her again. "You couldn't get those away from me, Lisa. They'll remind me of your visit. I'm just not sure I'm willing to share them with guests."

They talked until the fire died down, then said good-night. Adam took her hand as she headed up the stairs. "If you get cold..."

"You already sent two extra blankets upstairs, Adam. I'll be fine. I'll see you in the morning."

"Seven-thirty?"

"I'll be ready."

The next day she went to church with Adam and his mother. She felt none of the discomfort she had anticipated from going into a church. She didn't feel like the prodigal sister returned. She felt...at home. Throughout the afternoon she pondered Pastor Mike's warning that refusing to forgive others could hinder the ability to accept God's forgiveness of our own sins.

How easy it had been as a child to follow the

weekly ritual of going to Sunday school and the church service following. Why didn't she remember hearing such messages then? There was much more to faith than just going to church, she knew that. But as a child, they were one and the same. Even now she wondered how she could fit God into her schedule. With her life on the road, where she wouldn't have a home church, would she always feel as welcome as she had today? Or did that have more to do with Adam, or even her sisters, than she wanted to admit?

Adam pulled to a stop in front of the guest house and turned off the engine. "You okay?"

She didn't dare try to speak or he'd hear the emotion in her voice. She nodded.

"You go on in. I need to check the barn and get Toby from the kennel."

Once inside the solitude of the guest house, Lisa turned on the lights and saw the packet of photographs on the coffee table. She looked at the pictures again. It couldn't be. It had been nothing more than an act. Sure, she and Adam had become close friends, but...she looked again, unable to believe the tenderness in their expressions. They looked like a couple in love. It was impossible. One look at these, and her sisters would start planning the next Berthoff/MacIntyre wedding for sure.

She had to leave before matters got worse. Before she or Adam were hurt. No matter how she loved it here, Whispering Pines wasn't her home, and the sooner she left, the sooner her heart could return to reality. She blinked the tears away and hurried up the stairs to pack.

Toby raced into the room and ran all around before obediently sitting next to her.

"Hi there, Toby. How was your day?"

Toby's entire body wiggled and he barked as if he had an entire story of his own to tell.

"Is that so?" she said as she knelt next to him and scratched under his chin. "Guess what?"

"Woof." He lifted a paw to shake her hand.

Lisa obliged. "I have a job. I'm leaving tomorrow. I'm going to miss you."

Toby's long tongue stroked her cheek.

"A kiss for good luck. Thank you." Lisa hugged the dog, thankful for his unconditional love.

"When do you leave?" Adam's deep voice tremored as though some emotion had touched him.

"I didn't hear you come in." She forced a smile. "My flight's at 10:14 tomorrow morning."

"I didn't realize you'd leave so soon. Are you done with the Whispering Pines article, then?"

How could she tell him after all this time working on the story, she'd probably blown it? She'd gone against the editor's orders and wrote the article her own way. It wasn't Adam's fault. It had been her decision, her call. She knew the risk. "I'll finish it up tonight, but I'm not sure they'll use it."

"Wasn't that what all of this was about?"

"They want a different article than the one I wrote. I...couldn't write it their way."

He nodded slowly. "So, all this time..."

"I'm sorry I wasted your time."

He tucked his thumbs into his pockets and leaned against the doorjamb. "You aren't going to tell me they fired you, are you?"

She swallowed hard. Lisa turned around and opened her suitcase and began frantically throwing her clothes into the bag.

His voice lowered. "Lisa? Talk to me. Did they let you go?"

She went into the bathroom and tossed her shampoo and brush into the zippered bag. "They can't. I'm not an employee, I'm a freelancer. I'll send them the article. If they don't want it, tough." I wouldn't put it past Steve to bill me for the airfare, and never mind the full-time job. "I'll leave a copy for you to read, just as we agreed. Someone will love it, as is." The words came out softer than she'd hoped. She wanted to sound strong and confident. She'd done the right thing. There was no way she could betray the trust Adam had handed her. Adam didn't respond, and Lisa wasn't sure what to think. "Could I bother you to take me to the shuttle in the morning?"

"Here one day and gone the next. I hope you'll realize that nothing is going to fill the emptiness until you're willing to let it. You have to stop letting pain run your life. It's your choice to make a change, Lisa."

She couldn't face him, or the truth. She simply needed to leave. At another time in her life they might have stood a chance of finding common ground. But now she had an opportunity to break into a wonderful career and she couldn't turn that down. Adam was right, she still hadn't learned to let go of the past. She still hadn't gotten over her father leaving or Dale's betrayal.

Without warning, Adam's hand closed over her right shoulder. "I want your promise that you'll come back. I need you here to help me through the party. Your sisters need you."

Her sisters? She turned to him, bothered by the pain in his gaze. "I'll be here, Adam." She turned away and stuffed a few more things into the suitcase.

"There's no way all of that's going to fit. Leave whatever you'd like. I'll make sure it's safe."

Of course he would. Adam wasn't going anywhere. Adam was tied to this land. To his ranch. To his family. They were all around him, ready to come when he needed them. No one had ever needed Lisa. They were the ones who had taken care of her. "Thanks." She went to open the last drawer and paused. There was no way she was going to pack her personal things in front of him. "I'll be down in a while."

She watched his broad shoulders ease sideways through the doorway. "If you need any help with your bag..."

"I'm used to dragging the thing around, but thanks anyway."

"Come on, Toby. Let's get chores done."

Adam never dreamed love would find a place in his heart again. Especially not with the spunky sister of his sisters-in-law. Definitely not with a drifter.

In a week, Valentine's Day would be over, and Lisa would be on the road again, permanently. He tried to convince himself that life would go on without her, just as it had before. He wanted to believe that she would come back to visit. He wanted more than anything to ask her to stay, to never leave. You don't ask the wind not to blow, especially not in this area.

"We've only really known each other a few weeks," he muttered as he refilled the grain trough. "If I asked her to stay now, she may never come back."

"What are you grumbling about?" Lisa snuck up behind him. Adam spun around. She touched his wind-burned cheeks and warmed his red ears in her mittened hands. "You should know better than to stay out here all afternoon without something on your ears."

"You beat any hat I can think of."

Lisa smiled. "I made some hot chocolate."

"You shouldn't be out here. Your skin is more susceptible to frostbite than before." He led her out of the barn and motioned her toward the lodge. "I have time to take a break. What's going on?"

She bit her lip. "A break? You've been out here for hours. Dinner's going to be ready soon. I used the chicken from the freezer. I hope you don't mind."

"Why would I mind?" He watched her bounce ahead of him, and stepped up and took her by the waist. "How are the boots working?"

"Fine. They're toasty." She pulled away from his embrace. "Thought you wanted to hurry inside."

Adam watched Lisa run playfully through the snow. She stopped, rolled a snowball into her hands and tossed it at him.

"Feeling brave, are you?" There was a restless energy about her movements.

She leaned down to gather another snowball, a wide smile tantalizing him. Adam rushed forward just in time to get the half-formed ball in his face. He pulled her into his embrace and pressed his cold, wet cheek against hers. "You're pushing your luck."

"You're not going to retaliate?" Amusement sparkled in her blue eyes.

"Have you forgotten you were caught out in a storm less than a week ago? No, we're not getting into a snowball fight. Not now anyway. But rest assured, I will get even one day." He wanted a lifetime of snowball fights, teasing and getting even. He wanted her here, by his side, sharing his home. *Why, God? Why are You taking her away?*

Trust Me.

Adam kissed her rosy lips and turned her around, pushing her toward the lodge. I'm going to miss you so much. It made no sense. Lisa had only been here a couple of weeks.

He stomped the snow from his work boots and followed Lisa into the mudroom. What would she say if he confessed his feelings? Would she run, or would she stay? *I'm trying to be patient, God. Honest, I am.*

If God meant for them to be together, He would work things out. Adam had no doubts about His grace. God wouldn't close the door to Adam's personal life so tightly for all these years and open his emotions to Lisa so suddenly without a definite plan. Adam had to push his own desires aside and trust God's timing.

"I'm going to go clean up. I'll join you in a few minutes." Adam didn't wait for Lisa's response. He needed to be alone. He closed the door between the lodge and his house and collapsed against the log.

It was the one thing he struggled with—trusting people, trusting his own decisions, trusting God's plan. And right now, finding the love of his life topped his list of doubts. How could he have fallen in love with a woman who had no home, no roots and denied needing anyone, including her own family? How could three brothers fall in love with three sisters?

Chapter Twenty

The next morning Lisa looked at the time and rushed down the stairs with her camera bag and a small suitcase. "Adam!"

Silence.

"Adam." She tossed the article onto the table and ran outside just as he stepped into the barn. "Adam, we're going to be late."

He turned around, checking his watch as he latched the door. "I thought you said your plane left at ten-something."

Lisa ran to the truck. "It does. But I have to be there an hour ahead, and it's a three-hour drive...."

Adam took her bags and lifted them into the bed of his truck, then cradled her face in his hands. "Relax. We have plenty of time. It only takes about two hours to get there. Have you had breakfast?"

"I'm not hungry," she insisted, hoping her stomach didn't protest too loudly. "I can grab something at the airport."

He looked at her skeptically then handed her the keys. "I just want to say something before we leave."

She looked into his deep brown eyes, frightened by what she saw there. "We agreed to keep this simple. Don't ruin the wonderful time we've had by saying—"

"Ruin? What makes you think I'm about to ruin this?" His hand tenderly touched the nape of her neck and he paused until she lifted her lips to touch his.

Each time Adam kissed her she found her feelings for him intensifying. She staggered, alarmed that he steadied her. "Don't...don't say it."

"Say what?" He challenged with a stubborn set of his jaw.

"Don't make promises you can't keep, and don't ask me...to stay. Please." Her heart raced with need to move on. She'd stayed here too long, let down her guard and allowed Adam to expose her vulnerability. "We agreed. You knew this day would come."

Adam's eyes held hers captive. "When you're ready to stop running, I want to be the one you run to."

She shook her head. "I'm..."

"Running," he finished.

Lisa paused, afraid that if she blinked, this dream would disappear. She had spent a lifetime avoiding pain and commitment. Searching for something to fill the emptiness.

Could Adam have been right? Was she afraid of the one thing that could heal her heart? Love.

Adam bowed his head. "What I want to ask you...is to come back, as soon and as often as you'd like."

She blinked back tears, shaking her head, pleading for him to stop giving her false hope. What had happened to change the rugged cowboy's mind? They both knew all along that she would leave. They'd agreed to keep it simple. "You don't know what you're saying, Adam. Sometimes I'm on the road for two...three months without a break."

"I didn't say I wouldn't miss you." Adam kissed her. "Or that I might not want to join you once in a while." He took her into his arms and held her close.

Lisa felt the rise and fall of her chest. "Adam. I don't make promises, and I don't ask for them." She'd picked herself up after broken promises before, and wasn't so sure she was willing to do so again. "You knew I couldn't stay. You agreed..." A tear trickled down her cheek. Her hand cupped his chin. "You know I don't believe in promises."

He smiled. "Maybe you never found the right man to give you one. I can't avoid it forever. I won't. As much as I wanted to deny this could ever happen to us, I won't ever regret it."

"But this job—" she saw the want in his eyes "—is one I can't pass up."

"I wouldn't ask you to. One day you'll be ready to slow down, and I'll be here, waiting for you to come home."

Lisa wanted to stay in the security of Adam's embrace forever, yet duty pulled her away. He didn't understand at all. She couldn't give in to failure. Nor could she, like her mother, allow a man to take care of her. Lisa had to work, always would. If for no other reason than to have a safety net, something to fall back on—in case things didn't work out.

The emotions he'd woken in her were something she'd never regret and never fully understand. "I have to go, Adam. Please don't make it so difficult." She forced herself to smile. "I'll call."

"I promise that Whispering Pines won't ever be the same without your bright smile. Every time I look at those candles, I promise to think of the light you bring into my life. At that silly stuffed moose and beaver, I'll remember..."

Lisa closed her eyes and pain consumed her. "Adam, don't. Please don't do this to me."

He wrapped his arms around her. "What's wrong?"

"You're so sure of where you belong in this world. You are this land and this land is you... and I—"

"Would love to find out if Whispering Pines is where your roots can grow. So would I, Lisa."

Lisa closed her eyes, feeling her heart beat faster and faster against Adam's chest.

Adam rested his hand on her back. "It's okay. Calm down, take a deep breath. It's nothing to be afraid of." He breathed a kiss into her ear. "I'll be here when you're ready to make that decision."

"Adam, this wasn't supposed to happen...."

Adam's kiss erased the words from her lips and her mind. The winds blew, whispering that same soothing melody through the snow-capped trees. The breeze cooled her flushed face.

"You're wrong, Lisa. God brought you here. He woke those dreams for you and me again. One day, you'll come back. And you'll want to stay."

Lisa watched Adam and Toby disappear inside the lodge while she slid into the driver's seat, memories assailing her. She pumped the gas pedal, turned the key and the huge engine roared.

Lisa moved to the passenger's seat. It was time to face reality. After next week, nothing would be the same. She'd be busy chasing down the next job. He'd be tied to his ranch, making more people happy, changing their lives with his hospitality and his faith, just as he had hers. They would see one another at family dinners a couple of times a year. By then, he'd have a girlfriend or maybe even a wife.

Lisa shook her head. She couldn't think of that now. She had a lucrative job ahead of her, and if she did well, it could turn into a recurring commitment. It may not be journalism, but it would pay the bills quite nicely.

She would have plenty to keep her busy this week,

if she could just keep her wits about her for three more hours. Warm air pumped into the cab and Lisa looked at her watch. What was keeping Adam?

The door to the lodge slammed, and the sight of Adam made her heart race. It was this assignment, she decided. Romantic getaways. She'd been a skeptic when she arrived. After all these years, Lisa had convinced herself that romance was nothing more than an illusion. It had been, until Adam MacIntyre.

He climbed into the truck, put it into gear and headed down the lane. "You going to stay clear over there?"

Lisa's took in his powerful presence, noting his outstretched arm waiting for her to move closer. She scooted over, leaving plenty of space between them.

If Adam noticed, he didn't say anything. He rested his arm on the back of the seat and placed his hand on her shoulder. "So what's the plan with this exboyfriend of yours? You going to look him up?"

Did she detect a twinge of jealousy in his voice? "You don't exactly look up someone like Dale. It's more like tracking him down." She inhaled deeply, filling her lungs with the woodsy scent of Adam's aftershave. She dragged her mind back to the conversation. "I want to move on, Adam. I don't want to be bitter and unforgiving."

The truck bounced along the rutted road. He pulled her closer. "I want you to be careful. If he's out of jail, don't go looking for him alone. Okay?"

"I know what he did was terrible, but he wouldn't hurt me." Why was she defending him?

"Excuse me. He already did hurt you. It's beyond me why you ever stayed with him in the first place."

"He taught me so much about photography, I hoped I could—"

Adam cleared his throat. "You can't change a horse's color. He'd only abuse you again."

"He didn't abuse me."

"Use, abuse, what's the difference? His back's against the wall over whatever just happened to get him in trouble with the law. He's not going to be happy to see you all of a sudden, being that you have evidence to bring more charges against the man."

Adam wasn't just worried, he was on the verge of jealousy. "I'm not tempted in the least to go back to Dale." She smiled. "But I do need closure."

Traffic was heavy on the interstate, another reminder of what she'd left behind at the ranch. Lisa had forgotten there was a world beyond, with its buzz of traffic, and life without schedules and deadlines tripping one over the other. For a few blissful days, the world had slowed to a snail's pace and Lisa had seen the endless possibilities of life outside the perimeters of the lens of her camera. Suddenly the snippets of time she caught on film couldn't do justice to the intensity of the real life within them.

A few miles down the road Adam pulled off the freeway to fill the truck with gas and grab a quick breakfast. She ordered an egg, ham and cheese croissant and a large juice, and Adam ordered sausage, egg and cheese biscuits and coffee.

While they waited at the drive-up window, Lisa told him she'd left her computer and most of her luggage in the suite. "I hope you don't mind. I'm really not going to have time for much else this week, so it seemed silly to bring everything."

"I offered." Adam paid for the food, tossed the change into his ashtray and handed Lisa the sack. The welcoming smell of breakfast filled the cab. Fresh bread. Ham. Sausage. Coffee. The aroma crowded all other thoughts from her mind and sent Lisa back to the comfort of meals with Adam.

His voice burst into her dream like a pin into a balloon. "So if you don't have an apartment someplace, where do you keep your photos and files? What if another magazine wants an article while you're gone?"

How could the man think of such practical things right now? Lisa lifted the food from the sack and opened Adam's for him while she collected her thoughts. "All my stories and photos are archived on an electronic storage site. That way I can access them from any computer. It saved a lot of money replacing the laptop. I didn't have to worry about buying so much memory for the computer to handle all my files."

Adam seemed to chew on all the information as he finished his bite. "You keep your car and other belongings in a storage unit somewhere?"

"This really bothers you, doesn't it?"

He lifted one shoulder. "It doesn't bother me. It's totally beyond my comprehension." Previously occupied with driving and eating, he balanced the biscuit on his thigh and paused for a drink of coffee. "And I know how it would upset your sisters."

Lisa rubbed her hands on her jeans and to stall, took a bite of the breakfast croissant. Instead of moving to another subject, Adam waited. She'd have to face the issue. "I sold my car to stay afloat those first few weeks. It wasn't much, but it did help." Sipping her juice, Lisa felt the emotion of the experience return. "I rent a car when I need one. I don't have to worry about storage, insurance, upkeep or having it at the right place when I need it. It was an adjustment, but I'm making it work. Same with an apartment. Think of all the money that would have been wasted while it sat empty. After Dale, finding a trustworthy roommate seemed impossible."

"What about now?" Adam asked as he took the last bite of his sandwich and wiped his mouth with the napkin. Within seconds, his arm was around her shoulder again.

What was Adam asking? She felt her hair glide through Adam's fingers and words froze on her lips. She didn't want to know what he meant. She had to say goodbye in less than two hours. If he answered, she might not be able to get on that plane. "Right now, I need a job—" she closed her eyes "—before

I can even think of settling in any one place. If I'm going to continue freelancing, I don't need—''

''You need a home as much as anyone, you deserve it more than anyone and you want it more than you're willing to admit.''

Lisa took advantage of the chance to distract herself when Adam turned onto Pena Boulevard and continued toward Denver International Airport. She thumbed through her notes and found the information on her flight. She looked up at the signs and found the airline name. ''Go to the west gates. You can just drop me off. I know you have to get back to work.''

Keeping her distance was impossible as the huge truck rounded the many curves. Adam didn't seem willing to ease up on the gas pedal, which didn't help matters much. ''I'm walking you to the gate and waiting until the plane takes off.''

Adam pulled into the second level of the parking garage and immediately found a space. He shut the engine off, then turned to face her. Lisa tried to ignore the play of emotion in his gaze and failed.

He opened the door and pulled her out after him. Panic rose within her and all she could think of was to fill the silence with words. ''I asked Emily to come get me. I hope you don't mind, but I figured she and Kevin will be coming to the party anyway, and you'll have plenty to do....'' Each word tumbled from her mouth faster than the one before it.

''Whoa.'' He bent his head down to hers, his kiss

stopping her superfluous explanation. "All I want to know right now is that you'll be back."

She couldn't open her eyes for fear that he would see through her brave facade. Lisa nodded. Reluctantly she pushed herself from his embrace and turned her back to him. Through blurry eyes, Lisa glanced at her watch. "I'd better get checked in, make sure there are no complications with my ticket."

They rode the train to the concourse in silence, as if both dreaded saying goodbye, and finally came the announcement they'd both dreaded to hear. "Boarding flight 454 for Jackson Hole, Wyoming, rows 25..."

Adam took her into his arms for one last embrace.

Lisa gave him a quick kiss and turned, forcing herself to walk away. *Help me make it to Wyoming without falling to pieces, Lord. Please.*

"I love you," an emotion-choked voice whispered behind her. Lisa felt a moment of pause before she stepped up to the ticket counter and greeted the agent. You're imagining things. Keep moving.

Thirty minutes later, the airplane still hadn't taken off, prolonging the agony of her curiosity. Was the voice she'd heard Adam's, or another passenger's?

The flight attendant announced that they were waiting for weather clearance in Salt Lake City. Lisa leaned forward and looked out the tiny window toward the waiting area. Adam stood inside, watching and waiting, worry etched into his handsome face.

She closed her eyes and leaned her head against the seat. From her backpack, Lisa pulled out the small book Adam had given her that night after dinner. She opened the front cover and read the words that had caused her to toss and turn for two nights.

His arms are always around you, His word is always within you, His grace always covers you.
This week has changed my life.
Thanks.
Adam.
Ecclesiastes 4: 9-12.

For the first time since receiving the gift, she had the courage to see what verse he'd earmarked.

Lisa opened the Bible to the table of contents and looked up the book of Ecclesiastes, then turned to the verse and read, tears welling in her eyes. "Two are better than one, because they have a good return for their work; If one falls down, his friend can help him up. But pity the man who falls and has no one...two lie down together, they will keep warm. But how can one keep warm alone? Though one may be overpowered, two can defend themselves. A cord of three strands is not quickly broken."

Chapter Twenty-One

Lisa never wanted to fly again. After two delays at DIA, a detour around a winter storm and enough turbulence to shake the sense out of anyone, she finally landed at the tiny Jackson Hole airport.

Nevertheless, Rashke, the managing editor, wanted to put in a few hours, citing the importance of getting the kids back to work as soon as possible.

Lisa picked up pizza and delivered it to the set, hoping it would set them all at ease. Before all was said and done, they'd put in a five-hour day. By the end of the evening, Lisa was happy to have that first meeting out of the way. More importantly, she hoped the kids would be ready to have fun working again the next day. She went back to her room and collapsed on the bed.

How quickly she remembered just why fashion photography paid so well. These were children, and she was worn-out. She could hardly imagine the stress involved in working with prima donnas.

She made a quick phone call to Adam, glad to hear his deep, calming voice. Activity at the ranch had stepped up as the committee began decorating for the masquerade ball. He asked for her advice on whether he should order flowers, and Lisa had to admit to feeling a bit envious about Adam spending the week with Tara at his side.

"Your sisters are coming tomorrow to help out," he added, and Lisa noted an underlying tension in his voice.

Why would they get involved? "Isn't this a city event? I know they're coming to the party, but..."

As if he could read her mind, Adam finished the question for her. "They insist on helping."

"Everything's going okay?"

"Everything except that I miss you."

She closed her eyes and blinked away the tears. This was the grand opening. Professionally it meant everything that this go well. Personally it was a statement of his faith in God. "I'll be there, Adam." She wondered again if she should have left in the first place.

"You'll be my hostess, won't you?"

She let out a gasp and her heart beat faster. "My flight is scheduled for early Saturday morning. I'll come directly to the ranch." Lisa took a deep breath. "I promise."

"That's a pretty strong statement."

It was one she hoped she could keep. After all the delays she'd had on today's flight, she had her doubts. Flying had never bothered her before. Delays didn't usually stress her. Leaving had never been so painful. And landing had never rattled her. Today, all that had changed. Today, she'd left someone she cared about. Today, he'd asked her to come back. Today, she was needed.

His voice lowered. "Are all of your days going to be this long? You will call, won't you?"

"If you don't mind if it's late. After we're done shooting, we'll go to the office, develop the chromes, reevaluate the project and plan for the next day. We don't have the luxury of time on this one. Dale set them weeks behind."

There was a long silence. "It was him, huh?"

"Yeah." She said softly. "The stories aren't pretty. I can't believe it's the same man. Sounds like he's dug himself a pretty deep hole."

"You be careful, Lisa."

I want you back, she heard in Adam's silence. "Adam, please understand why I have to be here."

"I'm trying," he said honestly. "I'm fighting a terrible urge to run away—right to the Tetons."

"Save a trip for sometime when I can show you the sights. In the meantime, what did you think of the article?"

The silence lengthened. She could hear papers shuffling on the other end of the connection. "Adam? You did find it on the table, didn't you?"

"Well," he said, clearing his throat, "I think Toby spent the day chewing on the story. I'll ask his opinion."

She felt a laugh rumble clear from her stomach. "He ate it?"

"I wasn't sure what all those scraps were, to be honest, but I haven't seen your story."

Lisa shook her head, envisioning Toby ripping her story to shreds. She only hoped the editor didn't share the dog's sentiment. "It's still on my laptop under Whispering Pines. Take a look and let me know tomorrow what you think." She yawned so loud that Adam laughed. "Oh, I'm sorry, Adam."

"It's okay. I need to call it a night, too. Talk to you tomorrow. Good night, Lisa."

She was unable to reach Adam the next night, but had a very short message waiting for her at lunch the day after. He said he'd been unable to find the article, and that he'd call back later.

The shoot continued to go well, but Lisa couldn't seem to keep the lid on her insatiable curiosity. With a few questions she learned that the team had been working a week when Dale started showing up drunk, leaving the models terrified of one wrong smile. Rashke gave him two warnings, then fired him. When she'd tried to remove him from the location, he'd gone into a rage. By the time the sheriff arrived, Dale had broken the equipment and added charges of aggravated assault and resisting arrest to numerous outstanding federal warrants.

In the quiet of the nights at the hotel, Lisa thought of the layers of paint being stripped away. How many layers of protection had she been wearing to keep people at a distance—hoping that would prevent another "Dale" from hurting her?

He was less than thirty miles away from the resort in the county jail, waiting for a hearing. Resentment welled inside until she couldn't sleep. It was time she quit letting him ruin her life. She deserved a chance to move on, to remove the old and put a new "finish" on her life. She requested a long lunch the third day and made the trip to town.

After showing her driver's license and explaining to the officer the circumstances of her relationship with Dale, Lisa was allowed to visit.

She waited nervously along with another handful of visitors. The inmates were escorted in. Dale searched the room and looked right past her. Lisa longed to run and keep on running, just as she had been doing. *One day, you'll be ready to slow down, and I'll be here, waiting for you to come home.* She wanted to do this for Adam, for herself, for them. And with God's help, she would do it.

She hesitantly raised her hand. Dale glanced at her, obviously puzzled.

He looked terrible. His curly brown hair was long and bleached. His face was overtanned, leathery and covered with a new beard. His looks alone must have terrified the children.

"Lisa?"

She nodded, unable to hide her shock.

He dropped into the chair and glared. "Took you long enough to find me."

She could see the fear in his eyes, despite his attempt to intimidate her. "I didn't look for you, Dale. Anyone who hasn't the decency to say goodbye doesn't—" She cut herself off, fighting to overcome the bitterness seeping back into her heart. She had harbored anger and resentment long enough. Her short time with Adam proved to her that relationships and family were far more important to her than all the "things" Dale had stolen from her. Compassion. Forgiveness.

He laughed. "You're a little late. There's nothing left."

Lisa prayed for courage to say what she'd come to tell him. "I didn't come for my things, Dale. You may have taken my belongings, but you didn't take my heart." This wasn't coming out right. The words sounded stilted, even to her.

He eyed her suspiciously. "So what are you doing here? Gonna bail me out?"

She wanted to laugh, but she couldn't. Her mouth was dry, and she longed for the bottle of water she'd locked in the cubicle outside. "I came to forgive you."

"Yeah, right." He roared with laughter and slammed his open hand on the table. "It won't do you any good to press charges. You can't prove a thing."

The guard looked over at them. "I don't expect you to understand, but you can at least hear me out." She took a breath and continued. "I want my life back. Freedom comes from forgiving."

He leaned close. "If you want to forgive me, get me out of here. We can make another go of it."

She saw the desperation in his eyes, the fear, the willingness to say and do anything to escape the hell he'd gotten himself into. She didn't answer.

"You know how sorry I am, how stupid I get. I didn't mean it."

How many times had she heard that? Still, she'd never seen him this low, groveling for pity. "Maybe it's time you get professional help."

He glared at her, raising his voice. "You're going to dump on me, just like everyone else."

"You've dug yourself into a deep hole, Dale. Even my love couldn't have saved you this time." She'd once thought if she'd only loved him enough, it would make up for the emptiness in their lives. "I can't rescue you anymore. All I can do is forgive you for hurting me. I knew even then that it was useless to look for my things. I knew you'd sold everything to support your habits."

"Yeah, Miss Goody-Goody. Ran back to your sisters, I bet, told them your poor pitiful story and let them take care of you. And you can't even give me one more chance."

She blinked back tears. "It's time you pay the consequences of your mistakes. Maybe this time you'll let someone help you, but that won't be me.''

He jumped from his chair and kicked it across the room, yelling profanities at her.

She stepped back, numbly watching in shock as he slugged the officer who tried to restrain him. Additional officers and the jailer piled in the doors, removing all the inmates. Dale was thrown to the floor and cuffed.

Visitors were rushed through the exit, and Lisa was detained again by the officer who had interrogated her before allowing her to visit. After spending another hour of trying to convince her to press charges, Lisa stood up. "My testimony wouldn't do you any good, Officer. I only came today to close this door. Pressing charges would not only be futile, but it would chain me to a past I'd just as soon forget. I don't want revenge.''

"I hope you succeeded, ma'am. As for Dale, he won't be free to bother you for a good long time.''

She collected her pack and walked down the marble steps to the curb. Lisa took a deep breath; the bite of the cold air on her lungs reminded her of Colorado. And Adam. She closed her eyes, comforted simply by the memories.

How had her life changed so much in three short weeks? She had no more doubts. She had fallen in love. What worried her more—the possibility of Adam asking her to stay, or Adam letting her go—she couldn't decide.

Chapter Twenty-Two

Lisa pulled on her hose and the hoop skirt, then slipped the Southern-belle-style dress over her head and turned for Emily to tie the bow.

"How are you doing?" Emily tucked a stray hair into the bun and put the tiara on her head.

"Ouch." Lisa scrunched her nose and removed the crown. "Why do I have to wear this thing?"

Emily took it from her grasp. "Because you're supposed to be the Queen of Hearts."

"I thought it was a Southern belle costume."

Emily snatched the crown from Lisa's hand. "And when you add a crown, you become a queen. Hurry up, we need to get it clipped on. Adam's probably wondering where you are."

Lisa ducked so Emily could reach the top of her head easier. "He probably won't even talk to me. I promised I'd be here early and the party has already started.'' Or maybe he wasn't talking to her because of what she'd written in that article.

''Trust me, he's missed you,'' Emily said.

''Right.'' Halfway through the week she realized she'd never erased the article that had been written to please the editors. Had Adam mistaken that one for the newer version she planned to submit? Lisa tugged at the bodice of her dress, wishing it were one of the high-necked Victorian styles instead. ''So, is Adam the King of Hearts? Or are he and Tara coming as bride and groom, like she planned.''

''I don't have a clue what he ended up with. He may not have had a chance to exchange it, he was so busy this week since Tara backed out.''

''She didn't! Why didn't he say something?''

Emily had a guilty look on her face. ''He's had a lot on his mind this week, Lisa. I'm sure that's why he's been so hard to reach.''

Kevin had assured Lisa on the drive to the ranch that Adam would understand her delay. And while she wanted more than anything to trust her brother-in-law, past history prevented her from blindly accepting any man's word. It made no sense that Adam hadn't called or left any messages.

Lisa straightened her costume, applied a pale pink lipstick and dug through her bag for the blush. ''I knew something would happen to make me late. I should have never promised,'' Lisa grumbled.

That one article wouldn't leave her thoughts. Why she hadn't deleted it, she couldn't say. Even as she wrote the assignment, her conscience had bothered her. She'd known all along that she couldn't send it.

Snow pelted the window of Millie's bedroom suite. She had offered the use of her house so Lisa could freshen up without feeling rushed. "You made it in time. Just relax and enjoy," Emily said.

"The snowplows have been here, but what about the caterers? Did they make it through the storm?" Lisa wiggled her hips, enjoying the rustle of the elegant black skirt against the satin slips.

Emily patted Lisa's shoulders, tugging the shoulders into place. "It's all under control. Are you warm enough?"

Lisa looked at the velvet-and-cameo pendant dangling around her very bare neck. "I'm sure I'll be plenty warm once we're inside with all those people. Oh, Emmy, why did I ever agree to this? And why didn't Adam tell me Tara backed out?" Adam needed her, and she'd let him down already.

"He knew you were busy and didn't want to worry you. It looks like love to me."

Love.

The mere word had terrified her three weeks ago. And experiencing the emotion was the furthest thing from her mind when she'd arrived. Yet since stepping onto Whispering Pines, she'd come to understand the meaning of unconditional love.

Love. Between Toby and Adam. Adam and his family. And most importantly, God's everlasting love. Was it also possible for Adam to love her, too? Or was she in for another disappointment?

If Adam was even speaking to her, she wanted to tell him exactly how she felt. A week back in the fast-paced lifestyle she was accustomed to had changed her perspective on everything. Money couldn't provide happiness or security. She knew that now.

Lisa slipped her feet into her sister's high heels and groaned. "I can't do this, Emily. I'll break an ankle."

Emily laughed. "You don't have a choice. The dress is too long to wear flats. Now for the gloves."

She reached out a hand to her sister, feeling the awkward binding of the long evening gloves. "Now I know why I never went to prom."

"One night of frills hasn't hurt a tomboy yet. You'll survive."

"A tomboy?" She hadn't heard anyone call her that in years. A smile soothed Lisa's rattled nerves as she recalled the look on Adam's face when he'd seen her in her leather skirt. "I think not." She held on to the hope that whether or not she truly fit the tomboy mold, Adam would accept her apology and love her anyway. She had to show Adam that she had changed, and she could change even more. She could give up her career and make family her priority.

Her week spent photographing the children had been a blessing. She'd never realized how much fun kids could be, let alone wished for a family of her own. Lisa thought of her father. She had a long way to go to understand how he could have walked out on his daughters and wife, but prayed that God would help her to reach the point where she could forgive him, as well.

Kevin hollered up the stairs, "It's time to go, ladies."

Kevin greeted his wife with a kiss and gave Lisa a smile. "Adam had better hold on to his hat."

Lisa's nerves were so tangled and her mouth so parched, she couldn't even come up with a snappy reply.

A few minutes later, Kevin pulled into the circular driveway and stopped. Red carpet had been rolled out over the layers of snow.

Twinkle lights outlined the lodge and the rustic chandeliers inside glowed through the large picture windows. From outside she could see red heart-shaped lights and more sparkles than on New Year's Eve.

"It looks like a winter wonderland. And look...oh my." A huge draft horse stood in front of a sleigh adorned with twinkle lights and giant jingle bells.

Emily pulled out her ornately adorned Victorian mask and held it to her face. Kevin put his top hat and a mask on and handed the keys to the valet. "Well, here goes. Put your mask on, Lisa. Now you see why my little brother has been difficult to reach."

Lisa pulled the satin mask over her eyes as they

stepped into the lodge. Her heart beat in her throat just thinking of Adam. She looked around, disappointed that he wasn't there to greet her. "He's done a tremendous job."

"Adam doesn't do things halfway."

Lisa stood in the foyer, and not seeing Adam anywhere among the crowd, she turned to Emily. "I need to get something. I'll be right back." Before Emily could argue, Lisa hiked her dress out of the way, took off the heels and ran up the stairs to her suite.

Lisa was shocked to find the door was open and her things were gone. Panic filled her. *He promised my things would be waiting. That they would be safe.*

She dropped the shoes and collapsed against the wall. How could Adam have invaded her privacy and removed all of her things? The satin skirt rustled as Lisa went into the bathroom and opened the mirror. Nothing. She rushed back to the wardrobe and opened every nook and cranny, hoping to find her laptop. Her clothes, her computer, her life—gone.

There's an explanation for this, Lisa. Don't get upset. She dabbed the tears from under the mask and inhaled slowly. "He wouldn't do this to me. Not Adam."

Lisa opened the window, poked her nose against the screen and inhaled again, hoping the icy pine scent would calm her nerves. There had been so many people downstairs. Adam hadn't been there to greet her. He hadn't called, hadn't left a message.

"Lisa?"

Lisa hit her head on the window as she turned toward Katarina's voice.

"What in the world are you doing?"

She straightened the tiara and closed the window. "Getting some fresh air."

"You just came inside. What's wrong?"

Fear tightened around her like a noose. "My things are gone."

"Adam asked me to move them into his guest room so they'd be safe. He didn't want them in here with the open house. You knew he'd need to show all of the rooms off." Katarina's usual cheery smile was filled with concern. "You didn't think he'd gotten rid of your things, did you? Why would he do that?"

Lisa shrugged. "It's a long story." And it wasn't the time to confess to her sisters what she'd been through in the past year. Maybe tomorrow, but not now. "I didn't really think Adam had taken them, but…" Suddenly it dawned on her where Lisa had said her things were—in Adam's guest room. Not at her sisters, or at his mother's—in *his* guest room. Maybe it would be okay. "I guess we'd better get down there, since I'm supposed to be hostess."

Katarina nodded, then tried unsuccessfully to bend over and pick up Lisa's shoes.

"An eight-month-pregnant body should not bend

that far, Kat.'' Lisa slipped them on, stifling the groan. ''Promise me one thing. After tonight, I never have to wear heels again.''

''Not even on your wedding day?'' Katarina smiled. ''You've fallen in love, haven't you?''

Lisa ignored her sister's ''I told you so'' look.

As usual, Katarina's cheerful optimism overshadowed her goading. ''You may have avoided that bouquet, but it's my guess that its magic sprinkled across the room onto both of you anyway.''

Lisa spun around and disputed her claim, accidentally spilling the entire story.

''I knew it.'' Katarina said, bubbling with excitement. ''Wait till I tell the others.''

Lisa followed her waddling sister down the stairs, trying quietly to tell her how premature Katarina's exuberance was. She came to a sudden halt when she spotted Adam across the room with Tara.

Chapter Twenty-Three

Adam shook Tara's hand from his arm. "Excuse me, I have guests to tend to."

"I'm sorry I wasn't more help, Adam." She clutched the sleeve of his tuxedo again.

He leaned close, so as not to be overheard. "More help? Canceling all of the arrangements a week before the festival isn't exactly what I'd call helpful, Tara." He took hold of her hand and pushed it toward her. "In fact, I'm not sure why you showed up at all, but to be very honest with you—I wish you hadn't. Since you did, I'd appreciate it if you would quit pretending we're together. Lisa is my date."

Tara's perfectly plucked eyebrows arched over her green eyes. "Then where is she?" she asked with cold satisfaction.

A movement on the stairs caught Adam's eye and his heart beat double time. Slowly Lisa descended the stairs, a look of uncertainty casting a shadow on her beautiful face. He had to talk to her. Now.

So many things had been left unsettled. She must have misunderstood his message. She hadn't called. He hadn't wanted to set the rumor mill prematurely in motion by asking her sisters for her phone number.

Adam stepped past his mother and her gentleman friend, dressed as Anthony and Cleopatra. "Adam, where is Lisa?"

He looked up, but she'd moved. "She's here, somewhere." Adam stood on his toes and looked for a beautiful blonde in a tiara. "I'm trying to make my way over there."

"Good luck," Alex said. "I've been trying to find Katarina for half an hour."

Adam glanced at his brother. "If you find them first, tell them to stay put." He couldn't believe they had this kind of turnout on a snowy night. The weather wasn't even bad enough to keep the greedy and curious Chance Carter away.

Leave it to his cousin to dive right in and try to get his hands on whatever belonged to Adam. He supposed it was good that Chance was here to see the enthusiastic response to the guest ranch's grand opening. Maybe then he wouldn't be so eager to buy Adam's family out and subdivide the ranch.

He caught the glimmer of Lisa's tiara and pressed his way through the crowd, but was stopped twice to receive congratulations from neighbors. By then, she'd disappeared again. He could hardly think with all the noise. Judging from the laughter, he'd say the party was a success. Though they'd set up a sound system for dancing, there wasn't nearly enough room. All of the antique tables in the dining room were occupied; the great room looked like nothing more than a corral on sale day.

"Adam, we have a problem. Toby's loose, and has a terrified couple cornered on the veranda. He won't come to me," his sister Susan whispered in his ear. So much for finding Lisa.

Two hours after the party started, Adam escaped into the kitchen, and there in the corner, were Lisa and Chance.

"Adam." Lisa's eyes lit up. "Finding you is about as easy as locating a needle in a haystack." She immediately left his cousin's side and ran to him.

"I see my cousin did his best to fill in for me." He nodded to Chance. "I'll be happy to find a date for you, if you need help. Unfortunately for you, Lisa is already spoken for."

Chance tipped his head to Lisa. "So she says. I didn't realize you two were together."

"Now you do," Adam said, his gaze locked on Lisa. "I'd appreciate a few minutes alone with my date."

Chance laughed. "Sure thing. We'll have plenty of time to work out details of this deal tomorrow."

"Time to exit, Chance. You've worn out your welcome."

An extremely pregnant Cupid walked by and tossed red rose petals at Adam and Lisa. Katarina peeked out from under the pink mask. ''I knew it.''

Adam held Lisa even tighter and a rumble of laughter escaped. ''I never would have believed it.''

Lisa giggled. ''What, the bouquet or my sister?''

''Neither.'' He shook his head, still laughing. ''I have a surprise.'' Adam motioned toward the door.

She wrapped her gloved hands around her body. ''It's freezing out there, not to mention it's snowing.''

''Come on. It'll only take a few minutes.''

She hedged. ''We have guests. You haven't started the tour....''

Adam looked to her sisters with a pleading glance. ''I had this planned for earlier, but...''

''Go ahead. We'll take care of the guests,'' Emily and Kevin said in unison. Silence surrounded them, and Adam led Lisa to the back door, setting his tuxedo coat on her shoulders. ''I have a warmer wrap for you at the front door,'' he said, hoping it would be quicker to get there via the veranda. ''I've been waiting all week to have a minute alone with you.'' Despite her protests, Adam coaxed her out the door.

''But you have a house full of guests. And what did Chance mean about working out the details?'' Her eyes filled with concern. ''What's he talking about?''

In silence, Adam went into the lodge and returned with a velvet cape for Lisa. He put his coat back on and helped Lisa into the sleigh. After seating himself beside her, Adam took hold of the reins and they began to move. Bells jingled in rhythm with the horse's gallop.

"We'll talk, Lisa, but I want to be alone first." He felt the curious looks follow them, even as the sleigh turned out of sight. He covered their legs with the heavy quilt and slowed the horse to a canter.

"I've come to realize there's more to life than this ranch." He looked into her eyes, pleading for understanding.

She stared at him, a look of amazement on her porcelain face. "And I've come to love the idea of settling down in a place just like this."

She'd have recognized Adam's miserable smile anywhere, even hidden behind a Clark Gable mustache. He shook his head and looked down. "You haven't a clue what it takes to run a ranch, let alone a guest ranch filled with strangers, Lisa."

"I do have a clue, and I'm not running anywhere. So why are you? What deal is your cousin talking about?"

"He's agreed to keep the guest ranch intact. I want to be with you. I don't want to tie you down to my responsibilities."

Lisa felt the tears trickle down her cheeks. "Oh, Adam…" She leaned into his embrace and lifted her gaze to his. "Whatever made you think…" Her voice faltered. "You didn't call, and when I called here, you didn't answer."

"I worked until the wee hours of the night, cleaning, decorating...trying to keep my mind off how much I missed you. And then I lost your number." The sleigh had all but stopped. "Besides, from that article you wrote, I wasn't sure you really wanted to return to Whispering Pines. I figured I'd better do what I had to in order to keep you."

She hoped he didn't mean what she thought he did. "There were two versions of that article. Exactly which one did you want me to give an opinion on?"

Lisa pulled the mask from her eyes. "I wrote the one when you wouldn't answer any of my questions. I thought I'd deleted it."

"Does the article portray all of your feelings?" Adam's face didn't give her a hint as to how he felt about the article.

She faltered. "Which part, exactly?"

"The cowboy part."

Lisa tried to hide her smile. "You mean, 'the view is breathtaking, the food divine and *then* there's the cowboy' part? It really isn't a very well-structured sentence. If I were going to sell that story, I'd have to fix—"

He smiled. "Just answer my question."

Lisa nodded. "Even when you're angry and stubborn. I think I love you...." The words lingered like snow gently falling from the midnight sky. Adam took her into his arms and kissed her soundly.

"Adam...don't you dare give up this ranch for me or anyone else...."

He pressed his finger to her lips. "Hush. I've spent all week rehearsing this." The horse continued to the top of the hill overlooking Whispering Pines. "You have yet to see springtime in the Rockies, Lisa, but I can't begin to tell you how you remind me of a delicate wildflower, strong, determined and ever so beautiful."

She started to protest and he stopped her.

"No matter where life's journeys take you, I'd like you to always return to Whispering Pines. The roots of wildflowers grow deep into the rocky soil. If you'd like, this ranch could be your home." He reached into his pocket and pulled out a modest diamond ring. "If you would have me, I'd like to be your husband and I'd be proud to have you as my wife."

Lisa closed her eyes and pressed her lips to his, savoring each and every moment. "Yes, I'd love to be your wife."

In the distance Lisa heard a deep bark. She turned around and saw the cuddly black dog lumbering through the snow toward them. He jumped into Adam's lap and smothered both of them in kisses.

"And, Adam, I'd love nothing more than to come home to you and Whispering Pines. This time, forever."

Epilogue

"Francie, listen to me. For the last time, I'm thrilled that you liked the article, but I don't want the job. I'm getting married. I assume this means you're not coming to the wedding?"

"It's today? Oh dear, no, we couldn't get off right now." Lisa could hear papers shuffling on the other end. "I don't suppose Adam would go for separate houses. We'd really like you to join us here in the California office, but you'd have to agree to keep your 'Romantic Getaways' column." Her editor's voice turned dramatically throaty. "Think of it... An all-expense-paid honeymoon every month. Readers loved your feature on Whispering Pines."

Lisa nodded to her future sister-in-law and Susan pinned the veil to her hair. Katarina stitched Adam's grandmother's handkerchief to the inside of Lisa's slip and her mom adjusted the satin bow of the elegant wedding dress. Emily took the strappy sandals from the box and set them at Lisa's feet. "Francie, I really need to go now. I'll have the column in your mailbox by the deadline—don't worry."

Liz took the cellular phone from Lisa's hand and held it to her ear. "Excuse me, Miss Editor, but the bride is about to miss her own wedding. And if I know my brother, she won't be doing a lick of work for the next couple of weeks." Then Lisa's soon-to-be-sister-in-law pressed the power button. "Is that all I need to do to quiet this thing down?" She handed Lisa the bouquet of calla lilies.

"You look lovely," Millie said, smiling. "I couldn't be happier with Adam's choice of a bride."

There was a light knock on the door, and Lisa's grandfather poked his head inside. "You ready, dear? The groom is getting a bit restless."

"Almost, Grandpa." Lisa gave each of her helpers a hug before they went outside to be seated.

"Adam also asked me to help you with this." He stepped into the room and pulled a delicate wildflower necklace from a box. Lisa fingered it and opened the note that came with it. "I give you this flower, that our roots may continue to grow together."

Her grandpa's shaky hands handed it to Lisa's mother to put on. "I think you'd do better at this than I would." She put it on, and they walked out of her suite, down the stairs to the great room where Adam waited at the altar.

Pastor Mike performed the wedding ceremony inside the rustic gazebo, and Toby served as ring bearer. It had been six months, to the day, after Adam had walked into the church caked with mud.

After the formalities of the receiving line were over, Lisa and Adam took a minute to be alone. Adam kissed his bride's bare shoulder as they stood on the veranda watching the crowd. "I never believed anything could feel so right."

The shimmering white satin skirt rustled as she turned in unison with him; the guests' smiles reflected the joy she felt. "It was the bouquet, you know." She lifted her gaze to her husband's. "We should have listened from the start."

"Who says I didn't?" He placed his hand on her satin-smooth waist and pulled her closer as the music started. "May I have this dance?"

Adam carried her from the lodge veranda, across the yard to the specially designed gazebo. She stepped into the middle of the gazebo floor and lifted her hand to the stiff fabric covering his broad shoulders. "Could have fooled me. You didn't exactly give me a red-carpet welcome when I arrived."

Adam chuckled. "What did you expect from a cad?"

"I'm never going to live that one down, am I?"

He spun her into his arms and dipped her. "Not a chance. And we have a long, long future ahead of us."

Lisa giggled as he pulled her back up to meet his waiting lips. "Forever."

* * * * *

Dear Reader,

This book has by far been the most difficult for me to write. Don't get me wrong. I love Adam and Lisa, and the growth each must go through to find happiness.

The challenge in writing this story was the emotional upheaval in my personal life. Within the first six months of my deadline, I lost my dad, retired after fifteen years of child care, began an all-new career at the university and lost my father-in-law.

Needless to say, there were days I felt I couldn't go on, let alone pour my heart into my writing. There were days I wondered how I'd ever managed to publish a book, and days I wondered if I would ever really write again.

And then God sent me a perfect message through my characters: He does not want us to fill our lives with so many things that we have no energy for our families, our friends or Him. *Mark* 6:31 shows us that God wants us to take time to "veg out." He wants us to celebrate the joy of laughter. Our Father is compassionate, wanting us to enjoy time alone as well as the fellowship of loved ones.

For those who know me, this has not been, nor will it be, an easy concept to master. Slow down and take time to smell the roses, read a book, tell those you love just how you feel.

Carol Steward